THE ORPHAN PRINCE

MATTHEW J. SWARBRICK

CONTENTS

CHAPTER 1

*W*ar loomed on the horizon, casting a dark shadow over my once peaceful life. Little did I know how swiftly the tides would turn, thrusting me into a relentless pursuit of survival. A lifetime of chaos had condensed into the past year. Let me take you back to where it all began, a vivid memory etched in my mind. I was just eleven years old, blissfully unaware of the impending storm. France remained France, untouched by the invading Germans.

It was the early days of spring when my father and I rose with the sun. Our humble abode was nestled in a tranquil village in southern France, near the eastern alpine mountains. As the vibrant colours of nature emerged, the air carried the promise of warmth. Animals roamed with their newborns, and the anticipation of summer lingered. Today, I decided to visit the nearby stream, a perfect spot for fishing. Donning my boots and clutching my net, I ventured across the fields.

Before I could make my way outside, however, Father's voice halted me in my tracks. "Pierre, don't be gone for too long. I have important matters to discuss with you." I nodded eagerly, my mind filled with thoughts of fishing, and dashed out of the cottage.

The stream lay a short walk across the fields, where my father generously allowed our neighbour to graze their cattle and chickens. The arrangement meant we enjoyed free eggs and milk. As I playfully chased the wandering chickens, I pondered the purpose of my father's summons. I often assisted him with his carpentry work, but as far as I knew, he had no pressing need for my help. Although his workload had been light lately, perhaps a new order had arrived. Lost in contemplation, I reached the riverbank and settled on a large stone beneath the shade of nearby trees, their leaves rustling gently in the warm breeze. Crystal-clear water flowed before me, revealing glimpses of darting fish. Today held the promise of a good catch.

After several unsuccessful attempts, I finally hooked my first fish—a tiny common bleak. Yet, its presence suggested that larger fish lurked nearby. As I crouched closer for a better look, the sound of my father's voice reverberated through the air, calling me back for breakfast.

Reluctantly releasing the fish back into the water, I sprinted home, suddenly ravenous and apparently oblivious to the extent of my hunger. The aroma of breakfast wafted through the cottage as I entered, and without hesitation, I sat down to eat. Amid mouthfuls of porridge, my father began to explain the agenda for the day.

"Son, today will be different. I won't be heading to my workshop; I need you to accompany me to the lakes." I paused, spoon mid-air, my mind racing. The lakes? That could mean only one thing—fishing on a grand scale, far beyond the confines of our humble stream. Anticipation surged within me. However, as I eagerly awaited confirmation of my suspicions, my father's gaze met mine, which conveyed a different message. "But we won't be fishing today, Pierre. There are matters of great importance that we need to discuss." Disappointment washed over me as I looked at him, confused. "Listen to the broadcast," he said, getting up from the table and switching on the radio.

The room filled with the crackle of static, followed by urgent news about the relentless war which was ravaging Europe. The German forces posed an ever-growing threat, their aggression casting a long shadow over neighbouring lands. The broadcast revealed nothing new, just a continuation of the ongoing conflict. Struggling to comprehend the gravity of the situation, I turned to my father for answers.

"The war is drawing closer, my son," he explained, a sombre expression on his face. "The Nazi occupation will soon reach our borders. Our forces are no match for theirs. There is something I need to show you, and it's not safe to discuss it here." Confusion gripped my young mind. What did he want to show me? Why wasn't it safe? How did he know the Germans would attack when the news seemed to suggest otherwise? Questions tumbled forth in my head, but before I could ask any, my father silenced me, promising answers once we were far from the prying ears of the village. Then, with a knowing grin, he added, "And did I forget to mention? It's going to be an adventure, Pierre. Now, go and fetch the bicycles from the barn." An adventure. Excitement rekindled within me as I leapt to my feet, finishing my porridge hastily.

The barn, a vast wooden structure adjacent to our cottage, housed an assortment of my father's belongings, including his tools and a workshop. As I swung open the creaking doors, sunlight pierced the darkness and illuminated the treasures within. All actions became a blur as my father's plans seized control of my thoughts. An adventure with my father—what could it possibly entail? I swiftly retrieved my bicycle, ensuring the tires held good pressure and the chain remained intact. Why were we venturing to the lakes if not for fishing? I wheeled my bicycle outside and then returned to collect my father's. After conducting the same checks, I positioned both bicycles at the front of our house. Father awaited me, clutching two small sacks.

"We'll be gone all day, so I've packed lunch and dinner for us both. I've also brought your net, just in case," he said, a glimmer of excitement dancing in his eyes. Grinning, I mounted my bicycle, ready to embark on our journey to the lakes. The sun ascended steadily, casting its warm glow upon us. We pedalled past neighbouring houses, following the winding road that led us deeper into the mountains. The lakes were a couple of hours away by bicycle, a considerable distance from our village. As thoughts swirled in my mind, each possibility ushered in a renewed burst of energy, urging me to pedal faster.

Looking back now, I realise the immense difficulty my father must have faced, knowing that in a matter of weeks, circumstances would rip us apart.

CHAPTER 2

*S*till perplexed about what Father wanted to discuss with me, the journey felt like it lasted an eternity. I just couldn't wait to find out what it was. It must be really serious if he couldn't tell me at home. However, I loved travelling to the lakes; it was such a serene location, especially at this time of year. Everything appeared beautiful and crisp, with clear blue skies and warm, gentle breezes. The mountains remained large and ominous in the distance as we pedalled our way toward them. After what seemed like a century of time passing, we arrived at my favourite spot in the world. The lakes were a series of remote bodies of water formed over millennia from the constant rainwater running down the rivulets and tributaries from the peaks of the mountain range. Where there were crevasses in the valley floors, these beautiful lakes appeared and contained rare and interesting fish. Which was great for a day of fishing, although I then remembered what my father had said, that we wouldn't be going fishing today even though I could see my net protruding from his bag. Another feature of the lakes is their remoteness; they are quite tricky to reach, as there are no towns or villages nearer to them than our village. I think this is why they were my father's favourite place; he liked the peace and quiet they provided, where he could come and reflect.

As I thought I had arrived at our destination, I dismounted from my bike and turned to Father.

"Pierre, we are not there yet. We're going to the caves." He said to me.

The caves, situated in the valley side surrounding the lakes, are a large underground system of complex natural tunnels and spaces.

"Why the caves? Can't we talk here? No one will hear us." I responded, looking about at the completely vacant area.

"They won't; you are right. But there is something in the caves that I have never shown you before. Come on, let's go." I had no idea what my father was talking about as I watched him cycle on, but I was excited nonetheless and quickly pedalled behind him. In no time at all, I was at the small entrance which led to the complex system beyond. I turned to my father, following closely behind, and he beckoned me inside. Instantly, almost all light vanished as we entered these mysterious caves. The cool air could be felt on the back of my neck as I traced my hands along the jagged walls surrounding me. Drips echoed ahead as Father turned on his torch to light the way.

My father led me through the maze of tunnels, which felt like they would never end. We moved quickly, and I lost my bearings, but my father seemed to know the way.

"Just up ahead, son", he would say with encouragement every time I asked if we had arrived yet. When I stopped to ask again, he cut me off. "Look, do you see the light?"

I looked up ahead as he turned off his torch. Yes, I could see light; it was very faint in the distance but light nonetheless. I didn't think there was another entrance to these caves; we had explored them a lot, and I had never known of another way into the system. We moved toward the light, and a small expanse opened up in front of us. The light wasn't coming from an exit but a hole in the ceiling above. It was tiny, no bigger than the size of my hand, but it let enough light through to illuminate a small pool of water which had its own sandy shore, albeit only a few feet in length. Perhaps the opening was from an ancient well that had been mostly covered over the years, long lost over time.

"Ok, we're here," my father exclaimed.

"It's a very beautiful location, Father. Thank you for taking me here." I told him genuinely. It was particularly beautiful, but I wasn't sure why it was so important for him to show me this place. As if reading my mind, my father responded.

"Pierre, remember I said I wanted to show you something? Well, it wasn't something you might find in the natural." Pausing, my father struggled to articulate his words as he tried to explain what he meant. "It's better if I demonstrate."

Intrigued and perplexed, I watched my father wade into the pool towards a smooth rock face. The water rose to his waist as he pressed his hands flat against the wall above his head, his head bowed in reverence.

As I observed the wall, ancient markings and carvings came into focus, faintly illuminated by the light reflecting off the water. They depicted a complex array of symbols which appeared to resemble a map or celestial charts of some kind. Puzzled, I began to call out to my father, but my words trailed off as something unimaginable unfolded before my eyes. The smooth, glistening cave wall between my father's hands started to shimmer as if transforming into liquid. Ripples cascaded back and forth between his hands, and suddenly, a pinprick of light appeared amidst the shimmering surface. It expanded, radiating through the dim chamber, opening up to reveal glimpses of another world beyond our own.

Entranced, I involuntarily stepped into the water towards it; my eyes fixated on the enchanting portal. The circle of light grew larger, to the size of a bicycle wheel. Driven by a mixture of awe and curiosity, I waded closer; my hand outstretched to touch this mystical gateway. The opening stopped getting bigger, and I placed my hand through. I could see the light from the other side shining on my fingers and felt its warmth on my skin. I turned to my father, seeking guidance. He looked at me and grinned in excitement.

CHAPTER 3

*S*tanding in the dim chamber, I watched in awe as sunlight illuminated my hand, revealing a breathtaking forest beyond the shimmering portal. The chorus of birdsong and the gentle babble of a brook filled the air. It was a world of brilliance and wonder, a sight both extraordinary and supernatural.

I looked at my father with wide eyes, silently pleading to climb through into this magical realm. Sensing my unspoken question, he began to speak; his voice filled with a mix of excitement and tenderness. "Pierre, I brought you to this place to show you your true home," he said. Confusion clouded my thoughts as I stared at him, my mouth agape. "I would love nothing more than to walk with you through this portal and show you your true home. However, there is an ancient tradition in our family that prevents us from doing so until we come of age. But rest assured, this forest that you see, this place known as the Endless World, is where you truly belong. There are a few things I need to explain to you...

There exists a world that is not confined to space and time as the world we live in now does.

This Endless World, as it is known, never runs out of time. All living creatures eventually expire and return to dust in the ground. Those living in the Endless World do not age.

There is no end, and you could travel for all eternity and never reach its limits. If you set sail on the Endless World's many oceans, you would pass infinite lands.

This land is ruled by a royal family. They rule with kindness and peace. They govern and live to spread the ways of the Endless World to all around.

When a prince or princess is born, they begin their ministry on Earth to teach and bring about the ways of the Endless World. Earth is tormented by various plagues and adversaries, and it is the duty of the royal family to help steer those on Earth towards the righteous path to which they belong.

"Pierre, you are a member of this royal family, a prince. I'm a king, and your mother is a queen." my father revealed. I stared at him, unable to find my voice, grappling with the idea that this might be an elaborate joke.

"My mother?" I finally managed to utter.

"Yes, son. She resides in a magnificent castle beyond this forest," my father replied, pointing towards a trail within the wood, visible through the shimmering door in the rock. Tears welled in my eyes as I looked at him.

"Mother is alive?" I asked, my voice trembling with disbelief.

"Pierre, I'm sorry for not showing you this sooner. Traditionally, it is revealed once we reach adulthood. But yes, she reigns in the Endless World. As you know, she passed away during your birth. But those belonging to the Endless World will awaken there upon their departure from Earth," he explained, tears brimming in his eyes.

In the many days that followed, my father and I returned to the caves frequently. He became my guide, teaching me about the ways of the Endless World. He spoke of the perfect peace that prevailed, where conflict was nonexistent, and people lived in harmony despite their unique differences. They shared a common purpose, fostering a unity that Earth seemed unable to achieve. Together, we delved into countless discussions, exploring the mysteries contained within this parallel universe.

My father taught me about the portals that bridged the Endless World and Earth. He revealed the secret gift of being able to open these portals that our family possessed. It was our responsibility to traverse between the worlds, bringing the ways of the Endless World to Earth. Portals were everywhere, some hidden in plain sight, waiting to be discovered by those who understood the language of their surroundings. Nature held the key, with patterns and signs guiding the way. Branches pointing to a particular spot, sunlight revealing a hidden passage—it was all part of an intricate dance between the two realms.

Despite witnessing my father open one of these mystical portals, I struggled to replicate his feat. I would press my hands against the stone, hoping for a ripple or any sign of success, but nothing happened. Frustration gnawed at me, and doubt began to creep into my mind. Perhaps my father was mistaken, and I truly belonged only to Earth.

Undeterred, my father assured me that I would succeed. "Don't worry, son. You were born for this. It's part of who you are. Persevere, and you will get there," he encouraged me, repeating his words whenever he noticed my discouragement. While his words provided some comfort, I couldn't help but question my own abilities.

Our visits to the caves continued for several months, maximising my training. I treasured the quality time I had with my father; however, on what was to be our last visit, his demeanour appeared different, with a touch of sadness in his eyes. He beckoned me to join him outside the cave entrance, and as I sat down, he handed me an apple.

"This will be the last time we come here for a long while, possibly forever," he began solemnly. "A war is looming, and I have a duty to fulfil."

Confusion and anger welled up inside me. "But I thought we were here to teach peace, not engage in senseless wars," I retorted, the thought of my father leaving me behind caused frustration to surge through me.

"My boy, there are evil forces in this world, driving people to commit terrible acts. Sometimes, protecting others and fighting becomes necessary in order to achieve peace. War should be avoided at all costs, but when aggressors plan to perpetrate injustice, our only option is to fight and shield those who cannot protect themselves," he explained, his voice filled with regret.

I didn't want to hear his explanation; the thought of my father leaving me alone pierced my heart. I couldn't comprehend why such hardships were befalling us.

"Who's going to protect me?" I said to him, feeling a sense of betrayal. There was clear distress in my father's eyes, and I could tell he was fighting back tears.

"There is an orphanage deep in the mountains, run by a group of monks," my father continued, his voice laden with sorrow. "They care for children escaping towns and villages across the country. You will be safe there, away from the frontlines."

Tears streamed down my face as the reality of our impending separation sank in. "But what about you? Will we ever see each other again?" I asked, my voice filled with both desperation and hope.

"We will be together again, I promise you," my father said, his voice trembling with emotion. "Until then, remember who you are and the strength that resides within you. The monks will guide you, and they will teach you valuable lessons about compassion and resilience."

I didn't understand why this was happening to us. We had already suffered enough pain with the loss of Mother. Was I going to lose my father too?

CHAPTER 4

*S*nowflakes gently descended from the darkened sky as we stood on the vacant platform, awaiting the train that would carry me away from my father and towards the orphanage. We sought refuge under the shelter, observing the field on the other side of the tracks gradually transforming into a pristine blanket of white. In the midst of this wintry scene, I pondered how the once barren and unattractive landscape had been transformed into a thing of beauty. Yet, my heart ached as I considered the devastation the impending war would unleash, turning beauty into desolation.

"Pierre, I have arranged to visit you at the orphanage," my father whispered, breaking the silence. "I have discovered a nearby portal, not far from the orphanage grounds. To find it, you must cross the field behind the orphanage, find a stone wall with missing stones, and squeeze through. Head straight towards the wood that lies ahead. Within that wood, you will find a tree struck by lightning. There, within it, you will find a portal. I will leave you a sign when I arrive, and we can meet in secret." The news of the portal and my father's plans to meet me lifted my spirits. "It was actually the main reason I chose the orphanage to send you to."

I smiled at my kind father.

"It serves two purposes: one, for us to meet, but probably more importantly, for you to practice opening the portal and learning how to discover one. Fulfilling your royal duty is paramount after all — Earth's future literally depends on it."

"Through the wall and to the lightning-struck tree," I repeated, committing his instructions to memory.

"Son, I cannot stress enough the importance of secrecy. You must not breathe a word of this to anyone, not even your closest friends," my father cautioned, his gaze filled with seriousness.

"I understand," I replied, assuring him of my discretion.

"You should discover the portal and visit it whenever you can. It is crucial that you continue to practice. I know it may be challenging with the other children and the watchful eyes of the monks. You must learn to be discreet and create a routine that allows you to slip away unnoticed. Develop plausible reasons and stories if someone questions your whereabouts. I believe in your wisdom, Pierre. I trust that you will find a way."

Initially, panic threatened to engulf me as the weight of being separated from my father settled upon my shoulders. Without him by my side, I would need to navigate the complexities of life on my own. But as I reflected on his words, a flicker of hope ignited within me. I would be okay. I would find my way.

The snowfall grew heavier, and I wished that the train would never arrive, allowing me to stay in my father's comforting presence. Yet I reminded myself of the privilege that I possessed. Unlike the other children at the orphanage, I would have the opportunity to see my father regularly. Many of them would wait weeks, even months, for a simple letter.

And there were those among them who had never known the love and care of a mother or father. I began to feel ashamed as I acknowledged my own selfishness.

In the distance, I heard the mournful whistle of the approaching train. My father rose from his seat, gathering my meagre belongings together for me. A large single head-lamp pierced through the falling snow, revealing the grey outline of the train. Snow clouds billowed on either side as the mighty black snowplough effortlessly cleared the tracks, scattering snow back onto the platform. With a screech of brakes, the train came to a halt.

A heavy silence settled. Young faces peered out of the train's windows, momentarily curious about who would be joining them on this journey. Blank expressions watched my father and me. Their lack of smiles and warmth accentuated the difficulty of parting from my father.

"It's alright, Pierre. You will make friends, and the monks will treat you fairly," my father assured me. "Remember, you are going to a working orphanage, not only for evacuees, where some of the children have never experienced the love of a mother or father. Remember, the teachings of our Endless World benefit everyone. Treat them with kindness, and be slow to judge their actions. Just as you are a little prince in our kingdom, they too are little princes and princesses who deserve both respect and compassion."

Then, he tousled my hair, knelt down, and whispered in my ear, "We will see each other again soon."

"Thank you, Father," I murmured, my heart heavy I collected my belongings and boarded the open carriage. As the train began to move, I turned to catch one last glimpse of my father. His smile and encouraging wave filled my heart with both hope and longing. The man who had been shovel-ling the snow from the platform blew a loud whistle, signalling the train's departure. I watched as my father's figure grew smaller and smaller until he disappeared from view.

Stepping back into the now swaying carriage, I surveyed the faces of the other children. The fear and uncertainty I saw mirrored my own. Each individual kept to themselves, no one interacting with one another. Unsure where to sit or place my belongings, I searched for a place amidst this sombre atmosphere until my gaze met the eyes of a boy who stared back at me. With a silent gesture, he indicated an empty space in the overhead racks where I could stow my bag. I nodded with gratitude and secured my belongings, sitting in the seat which was available next to his.

"Hi, my name is Marc. What's your name?" the boy introduced himself, his demeanour starkly contrasting against the prevailing silence throughout the rest of the carriage.

"I'm Pierre. Nice to meet you. Have you travelled far?" I responded politely.

"I'm not from around here, but I've been staying with family in the town before your town," Marc replied with a hint of cheerfulness in his voice.

"Were you with your parents?" I inquired, curiosity piqued.

"No, I was staying with my uncle. My family is from Paris, and my parents thought it would be safer for me to come south. Turns out, safety may be elusive after all. But I'm sure we'll be well cared for at the orphanage."

Paris. The mere mention of the city stirred excitement within me. Though I had never been there, I had heard countless tales of its wonders.

"What's Paris like? I've always wanted to see the Eiffel Tower!" I exclaimed, full of enthusiasm.

"Paris is amazing, Pierre. Perhaps, once this ordeal is over, I can show you around. You can stay at my parents' mansion," Marc replied, his words tinged with a touch of grandeur.

Mansion? As I began to imagine it, the sadness that had weighed on me moments before began to dissipate with every passing minute. Not only had I already made a new friend, but the promise of a future adventure in Paris beckoned. Marc and I continued our conversation, sharing our backgrounds and stories.

As the train barrelled forward, carrying us into an unknown future, I couldn't help but feel a renewed sense of optimism. Little did I know, however, that the new friend I had chosen would lead me to the most unexpected challenges and the realisation that not everyone should be trusted. The lessons my father had imparted about being wise as a serpent and harmless as doves would soon become painfully relevant.

CHAPTER 5

I must have dozed off, as the screeching of brakes jolted me awake as we approached the next station. The darkness outside indicated that several hours had passed since our departure. The children around me rose from their seats, eager to catch a glimpse of the newcomers. We had reached a bigger town, and more evacuees were boarding the train.

Looking out of the window, I noticed two boys accompanied by a dishevelled man, presumably their father. His appearance was worn, with an unkempt beard, and he was clutching a bottle concealed within a brown paper bag. The man swayed unsteadily, his grubby toes poking out from his shoes. The boys, one older than the other by what looked like two or three years, stood cautiously, perhaps mindful not to provoke their father's anger. Suddenly, the man roughly grabbed the older boy by the neck, and his drunken words reached our ears.

"Toe the line, boy. I don't want to be traipsing over to this damn orphanage to sort you out. Do you understand?" he slurred.

Both boys nodded quickly, their fear palpable. "Yes, Father," the older boy replied, his voice filled with urgency. "We understand."

With a forceful motion, the man threw his elder son towards the open train door. The boy stumbled and fell, then scrambled to his feet to avoid further embarrassment. His younger brother followed suit.

The scene left us all in a state of shock, exchanging nervous glances. The train began to move, putting distance between us and the drunken father, and with it came a collective sigh of relief echoing through the carriage. As we departed the station, pity welled up within me for those two boys, and somehow I knew I wasn't the only one. Determined to extend the same kindness I had received from Marc, I stood up and approached them, ready to offer assistance with their luggage and finding vacant seats.

As I walked towards them, the younger boy maintained the same anxious demeanour he had displayed on the platform. It soon became evident why when the older brother aggressively grabbed him and, speaking in threatening tones, instructed him to find their seats. The younger boy nodded emphatically, his response laced with fear. "Yes, Eric."

The younger boy then made his way towards me in the aisle, unsure what to do. I smiled warmly at him and extended an invitation. "We have some seats here. Would you like to sit with us?"

He stared at me, uncertain. His gaze shifted back to Eric, waiting for instructions. However, Eric seemed preoccupied, rummaging through his bags. "Um, okay, thanks," the younger boy replied before scurrying back to his brother.

Eric glanced up, picking up his bag nonchalantly, and lit a cigarette, before following his younger brother over to our seats. I glanced at Marc, to see his reaction. I was certain that children were not allowed to smoke on the train. While I had witnessed the train crew smoking during their rounds, Eric's actions were a clear violation of the rules. Nevertheless, I remained silent, not wanting to escalate the tension further. The younger brother's fearful demeanour permeated the carriage, casting a shadow over the atmosphere.

"Hi there, are you Eric?" I asked as they approached, introducing myself. "My name is Pierre, and this is my friend Marc. We have two spare seats here if you would like to sit with us."

Eric scoffed, looking at his younger brother. "Do you own the train or something? I can sit wherever I want, mate. In fact, you'd be best off leaving me and my brother alone."

I had never encountered such rudeness before. Despite my intention to show kindness, Eric responded with aggression and malice.

"Calm down. Pierre was just trying to help," Marc intervened, standing up in my defence. His act of bravery was honourable, but a part of me silently urged him to remain quiet. Eric seemed like a volatile individual, capable of unpredictable actions.

"You better mind your own business," Eric retaliated. The entire carriage turned to observe the escalating confrontation. Marc stood his ground, unwilling to back down. Silence settled in the carriage, tension thick in the air. Then, as quickly as it had erupted, the confrontation dissipated. Eric turned to his brother, with a baleful grin, and nudged his shoulder. "He's a sensitive one, isn't he?" His brother responded with nervous laughter. Marc looked at me, slightly confused, while Eric slumped down into one of the offered seats and stared out of the window. What an odd boy he was. Relief washed over me as the encounter ended, and the rest of the carriage resumed their own business. Marc lowered himself back into his seat, and shrugged, exchanging glances with me.

We continued our journey through wintry landscapes, the carriage lights flickering occasionally. A big moon glimmered in the starlit sky, casting an otherworldly glow over the snow-covered surroundings. The snowfall had temporarily ceased, leaving everything adorned in a smooth layer of crisp white. We seemed like a ship gliding through clouds in the sky, carving our way through a sea of white.

Suddenly, the train plunged into darkness as we entered a tunnel. These tunnels must have been painstakingly excavated through the hard mountainous rock, and I couldn't help but wonder about the immense time and effort it must have taken to create these extensive tunnels. Memories of digging a well with my father in our village came to mind, particularly the laborious process we had undertaken. I marvelled at the dedication and perseverance required to accomplish such a monumental task.

The screeching of brakes brought me back to the present as the train exited the tunnel, slowing to a halt and immersing us in the welcoming light of the next station stop. I felt a sense of apprehension. Who would join us now? Would we encounter another Eric or perhaps someone even more challenging?

As expected, a similar scene unfolded. Everyone stood up, craning their necks to catch sight of the new arrivals. I joined them, my eyes drawn to a lonely little girl who stood nervously, clutching a single satchel. She couldn't have been more than five or six years old, wearing a simple bonnet and a neat school uniform. I couldn't help but wonder where her parents were, absent from her side during what was, for some, an emotional departure. As I contemplated her situation, I felt a sinking feeling. We were hurtling towards a time of uncertainty and conflict, and the thought of this young girl, evidently alone and abandoned, tugged at my heart.

She looked around, observing the other children with

their families hugging and kissing. She made no other movements, seemingly waiting for something, mirroring the actions of the other children as they slowly boarded the waiting train. Step by careful step, she traversed the snow-covered platform, heading towards our carriage. However, by the time she reached us, the last few remaining seats had been claimed. Each vacant chair was snatched away moments before she approached. My heart ached for this little girl.

Timid, she made her way to the doors at the end of the carriage and sat on the empty floor. Driven by compassion, I decided to approach her and offer my seat. "Hi there, my name is Pierre. You can have my seat if you'd like," I offered. She looked at me, then shifted her gaze towards my seat, where Marc, Eric, and his brother were all sitting. Quickly, she shook her head, her fear palpable. Sensing her hesitation, I tried to reassure her.

"I can come to sit next to you if you'd like. I don't mind sitting on the floor," I suggested. She paused, contemplating my offer. She glanced back again at the three boys and shook her head. I looked at my seat, where Marc had his eyes closed, likely sleeping; I wasn't particularly keen on engaging with Eric. "How about I come and join you here?" I suggested. She looked at me and smiled, squeaking a small "Thank you."

I returned to my seat, collected my belongings, and made my way back over to her. Sitting down, I asked for her name. "Isabelle," she replied, clutching her satchel tightly. Together, we stared out of the window that formed part of the carriage door, watching the dark snowy landscapes pass by as the train continued its journey deeper into the mountains.

CHAPTER 6

*E*mmerich Stahl lay in his bed, the bedsheets neatly kept, folded towels placed precisely on the chair beside the bed with a pristine newspaper resting on top. The room exuded an air of perfection, with paintings of romantic Greek gods and goddesses frolicking in fantastical landscapes adorning the clean white walls. The wall facing the end of the sleeping man's bed was a small fireplace with blackened walls where flames had licked them the night before. The ashtray, however, was empty and swept, ready for the new day.

As the youngest of four brothers, Emmerich felt the constant weight of their achievements pressing upon him. His siblings had excelled in various fields— one a successful businessman, another a renowned doctor, and the third an accomplished author. Their father, a former military general turned government official, had cast a formidable shadow. Joining the army was Emmerich's way of seeking his father's favour. He quickly rose through the ranks, and he now commanded an elite unit as a captain.

In his room, a small writing desk stood furnished with

various drinking glasses and decanters, which cast interesting reflections as the sunlight from an approaching dawn seeped through the gaps in the curtain.

With closed eyes, he seemed peaceful, waiting for the day to truly begin. However, beneath the facade of serenity, an ugly truth lurked. Above Emmerich's bed hung a portrait of Adolf Hitler. It did not reside there out of fear or duty, but out of a twisted sense of respect and admiration. This ideology that fuelled his aspirations for power was deeply ingrained.

As if responding to an internal clock, Emmerich rose from his slumber as the sun pierced the horizon. He carefully folded the sheets, attending to even the most insignificant details like neatness. This served as an example to the men he commanded of the type of soldier he desired, being untidy was despicable and grotesque. To him, commanding respect from his men in all areas was crucial, but more important than respect was fear. For Emmerich, fear was a tool of control, a means to bend others to his will. His men were mere stepping stones on his path to personal advancement.

His morning routine began with sixty press-ups and sit-ups, a gulp of water from the sink, followed by a meticulous clean shave and wash. Every action was performed with methodical precision, designed to maintain an image of authority. Putting on his captain's uniform, he ensured not a single crease disrupted the immaculate appearance. The boots, already polished as part of his nighttime ritual, completed his attire. Ready for the day ahead, he turned to the framed portrait of his ultimate leader, raised his right arm in front of him and religiously barked, "Heil Hitler!"

With the newspaper tucked under his arm, he left the room, heading for breakfast and the drills and exercises that awaited him and his unit.

The military base, located in a retired castle in Bavaria,

was divided into two sections. The common soldiers were stationed in the servant quarters and makeshift sleeping quarters within the grounds, while the officers, captains, and high-ranking individuals occupied the grand rooms of the castle itself.

Emmerich strode with confidence across the vast hallways, his footsteps marching on the ornate rugs and clean checkered tiling. He descended the grand marble staircase, flanked by towering pillars dressed with large red banners. With confidence, he entered one of the dining rooms and took a seat at a solitary table. Placing the newspaper before him, he savoured a steaming cup of coffee while a maid came to his table and, swiftly removing the lid from a metal cloche, revealed a breakfast of poached eggs and bratwurst. As he ate his morning meal, the marching steps of a soldier disrupted his repose. Annoyed, he dropped his cutlery to see who was responsible for the disturbance in the privacy of the officer's and other high-ranking officials' dining rooms.

A young private marched up to Emmerich's table, stopping, turning, and saluting, awaiting his captain's attention.

"Yes?" Captain Stahl retorted, his tone conveying the expectation of a swift and concise message.

"Sir, I've been tasked with requesting your presence at a meeting with Commander Berg and Commander Reinstadt. They want to meet with you first thing in their office, sir."

Emmerich's heart quickened. A meeting with his superiors could only mean one thing—recognition for his hard work and, perhaps, a promotion. Nodding subtly to the private, he rose from his seat, preparing himself for the encounter. The commanders' offices resided in one of the castle's three towers, offering commanding views of the grounds and the valleys beyond, ensuring that their soldiers remained aware of their watchful gaze.

Despite his strength and vitality, Emmerich gave himself

a moment before knocking on the door and entering the office. He refused to allow his commanders to perceive even the slightest hint of weakness. Three sharp knocks echoed through the room as he awaited permission to enter. Once granted, he adopted the same stance as the private minutes before.

"Herr Stahl, please take a seat."

Emmerich obeyed, settling into a simple wooden chair. The room resembled his own sleeping quarters, but instead of paintings of Greek deities, it was decorated with paintings of the German countryside and detailed maps of Europe, marked with pins denoting strategic locations. Two commanders sat on one side of a large writing desk, a deliberate arrangement leaving no doubt as to who held the upper hand. Behind them, pictures of their Führer and themselves mingling with influential figures in the German government served as a constant reminder of their gained power and authority.

"Herr Stahl, we are immensely impressed with your work," Commander Berg began, his words laced with a mixture of approval and expectation. "Your men have proven highly effective and have become a valuable asset to our nation. But your journey has just begun, and we see a major role for you in the ongoing war effort."

"Thank you, sir," Emmerich responded, concealing the inner disappointment that empty praise held little value to him. Words alone would not further his ambitions; he sought tangible progress and personal gain.

"An opportunity has arisen, and we are considering you and your elite unit to execute the operation," Commander Reinstadt continued, his gaze fixed on Emmerich. The prospect of advancement tantalised him, stoking the fires of his ambition.

"We need someone who is loyal, someone who will go

beyond what is normally required," Commander Berg added, his tone growing in gravity. "Many men can be loyal, but not many have the stomach to do what is necessary. We are at war, Herr Stahl and war demands actions beyond what is expected in everyday life."

Emmerich, keenly aware of his own capabilities and the lengths he would go to achieve his goals, responded without hesitation. "I am that man, sir. By any means necessary."

The commanders exchanged a meaningful look, silently conveying their decision. They had found their instrument, their man who would do whatever it took to achieve victory. "Herr Stahl, we need to ensure victory across Europe," Commander Berg explained. "We are advancing, but the Russians persist, and rumours of a British invasion circulate. To secure victory, we are exploring alternative means of warfare, including scientific breakthroughs. We believe we have discovered a weapon that will guarantee success."

Commander Berg handed Emmerich a brown envelope, its contents holding the details of the mission. "Read through it carefully, organise your men, and make your preparations. You will rendezvous with two scientists and their equipment at a secret facility that only the pilot will know. You will then take these scientists onto a remote area of southeastern France. The geographical importance of this region is directly tied to this new weapon, and it cannot be overstated."

Grasping the envelope, Emmerich stood and saluted his superiors. He understood the significance of the mission and the consequences if he were to fail. He had seen firsthand the fate of those who faltered or fell short. Treason meant execution, and he had no intention of meeting such a grim end. Nodding in acknowledgement, he made his exit, his mind already racing with thoughts of the operational details he would need to discuss with Johan Baumann, his second in command.

As Emmerich navigated the castle's corridors, his thoughts centred not on the mission's objectives but on how this opportunity could elevate him further on the path to power and success. The object of the mission ahead was secondary to his own personal advancement. The sacrifices required, and the collateral damage incurred, mattered little to him as long as his own objectives were achieved.

CHAPTER 7

*F*irst Lieutenant Baumann diligently led his unit through various military drills in the absence of Captain Stahl. Baumann was a devoted soldier, always following orders obediently, driven by a strong sense of duty. Unlike Stahl, however, he lacked the same competitive drive and personal ambition. Nonetheless, he firmly believed in fighting for his country and wholeheartedly embraced the vision set forth by the fascistic German government.

On the cold wintry morning, Baumann and his elite special operations unit embarked on their daily run around the castle grounds. The soldiers, weighed down by full gear— packs, rations, rifles, and pistols—persevered through the biting cold winds as they navigated around woods and a large frozen lake. Wooden targets of enemy soldiers were strategically placed along their route, allowing the unit to practise and refine their military skills. This particular unit specialised in rural warfare, with training exercises primarily focussed on operating in natural environments, mastering stealth tactics, and learning how to sustain themselves by living solely off the land. They were trained in the art of hiding in the snow, constructing shelters in the woods, hunting, and setting traps. Recent successes included a reconnaissance mission monitoring Russian movements on the eastern front, where such training and resilience proved invaluable when confronted by the bitter cold.

As the men completed their run, they returned to the barracks, seeking solace and warmth in their dormitories. Baumann barked orders for the next military exercise, "Prepare for military exercise eleven," before making his way to the office at the barracks. Military exercise eleven involved a coordinated attack on an enemy stronghold, employing both stealth and surprise tactics. Two snipers would provide cover from a makeshift vantage point while separate groups would execute a pincer attack, catching the enemy off guard.

Entering the office, Baumann anticipated a moment of respite as he prepared to enjoy his morning coffee and pipe. However, he was greeted by Captain Stahl, seated behind his desk, smoking his pipe, with an open envelope lying before him.

"Lieutenant, we have a new objective," Stahl announced, sliding the envelope toward Baumann, signalling for him to sit and read the contents. Baumann poured himself a cup of coffee and offered Stahl a portion, which he declined, instead choosing to puff on his pipe. Baumann began perusing the objective details, his eyebrows raised curiously.

"Herr Stahl, scientific research? Do we have any information about the nature of this research?" Baumann inquired, seeking clarity.

"Not more than you have already, Baumann. It's classified on a need-to-know basis, as you well know. Commander Berg and Reinstadt believe it will be a game-changer, guaranteeing victory. Initially, I saw it as a mere babysitting mission for a couple of scientists, but now, I must admit, I'm intrigued," Stahl responded with a subtle gleam of curiosity.

Together, they delved deeper into the particulars, poring over a detailed map of the route and region and strategising the best tactics to approach the mission. While the operation appeared relatively straightforward, the rugged mountainous terrain presented its own challenges, particularly with regard to limiting access to food supplies during the winter months. Nevertheless, Stahl's unit was always prepared for any situation, and they were ready to commence the mission immediately.

Stahl and Baumann set to work, making the necessary preparations for an imminent departure. They arranged for the use of the Junker Ju 52 transport plane from the nearby airstrip to facilitate their journey. Stahl, frustrated by the undisclosed location of the secret military facility near the Swiss border, would only receive the coordinates once they were airborne. After picking up the scientists and their equipment, they would fly to the Italian-French border, utilising German-Italian cooperation to access French territory and beyond into the Mediterranean. Their flight would take them through northern Italy until they reached the border, where they would land and proceed on foot through the treacherous mountains to establish their base. Once there, their primary objective would be to assist and protect the scientists conducting their research.

The preparations proceeded rapidly, as the men had learned to travel light and be well-drilled for any situation. Stahl had swiftly secured the use of the transport aircraft, and he led his men to the airfield, instructing them to complete the loading and prepare for takeoff. He left them momentarily, joining his commanders, who awaited him in their military vehicle.

"Herr Stahl, we neglected to mention a vital piece of information during your briefing. There is a small working monastery near your destination. We have a spy planted there who may prove to be a valuable asset to your mission," Commander Berg divulged, alluding to the possibility of better shelter than foxholes in the woods. "The monastery is currently functioning as an evacuee centre due to its remote location. Will this pose any issues for you, Stahl? It is of utmost importance that no one discovers the reason for this operation. Absolute discretion is required."

Stahl nodded, understanding the significance of maintaining secrecy and the potential consequences if their mission were to be compromised.

"Rest assured, commanders, I understand the absolute importance of discretion and will do whatever it takes to ensure the success of this mission," Stahl affirmed with a determined gaze.

The commanders exchanged satisfied glances before bidding Stahl farewell and driving back to the castle. Left alone again, Stahl's gaze shifted back to the waiting plane. The sound of the engines revving and the anticipation of what lay ahead fuelled his desire for success. He was ready to embark on this challenging mission, eager to put his skills and training to the test.

With each step he took toward the aircraft, Stahl's resolve hardened. He would do whatever it took to ensure the success of this mission and the success of his career.

CHAPTER 8

I awoke to the dimly lit interior of the carriage, the darkness enveloping us as we slumbered. The rhythmic motion of the train, accompanied by the low rumble of the engine reverberating through the carriages, created a soothing sensation. Isabelle, still clutching her satchel, lay curled up on the floor, lost in her dreams.

As I peered outside, I noticed that the moonlight struggled to pierce through the light cloud cover, casting an ethereal glow on the dark, mountainous shadows that surrounded us. We must be nearing our destination. The tranquillity of the surroundings and the stillness of the night calmed my nerves, and the thought of reuniting with my father kept me content. Despite the uncertainties that lay ahead, I began to see the upcoming adventure as an opportunity for growth, even though certain individuals, like Eric, could make the road ahead arduous.

Just as I was drifting back to sleep, the sudden flicker of lights jolted me awake, accompanied by the urgent entrance of a train worker into our carriage.

"Calling at the final stop in 5 minutes!" he exclaimed

repeatedly as he hurried through, making his way to the next carriage. The rest of the carriage groggily rose from their slumber, rubbing eyes and exchanging confused glances. My gaze fell upon Isabelle, who was clearly anxious and clutching her bag with whitened knuckles. I reached out to reassure her.

"Don't worry, Isabelle. You can stick with me," I said, hoping to ease her apprehension. I saw her grip on the satchel loosen ever so slightly.

Moments later, the screeching of brakes shattered the silence as the train approached its final stop. In that instant, I realised how much normality of life I had taken for granted until it was abruptly taken away. The doors opened, releasing an icy blast that invaded the warmth of the train, swiftly vanishing into the cold night. I tightly gripped my coat and scarf, helping Isabelle step onto the frosty platform. The pale glow of several lamps illuminated the scene, their feeble light flickering in the biting wind. Though there was no snowfall, the harsh gusts whipped up the settled ice crystals, stinging our uncovered faces. Up ahead stood a small building, presumably the station porter's cabin, constructed with a mixture of stone and wood. Thin plumes of smoke billowed from its solitary chimney, hinting at the comforting warmth within.

A group of hooded men in grey cloaks, presumably the monks, stood beside the cabin, their presence as still as statues. I found their lack of movement somewhat unsettling. Two horses and a large carriage were poised nearby, ready for departure. As I surveyed the platform, I counted the children present, realising that there would be at least two trips for the monks to transport all of us. It was a first-come, first-served situation. I contemplated making a run for it to secure a spot on the first coach but dismissed the thought as I looked down at Isabelle. We were holding hands—I don't recall when exactly I had taken hold of hers. The cold penetrated our clothing, causing intense shivering, and at that moment, a tempting voice whispered in my mind, urging me to let go of her hand and make a dash for the potential of warmth. But I stood firm, refusing to yield to it. It wasn't in my nature to abandon those in need.

The other children seemed to grasp the situation before them, prompting a frantic rush toward the coach. Their desire for warmth heavily outweighed any sense of hesitation. The porter shouted warnings as children slid and stumbled across the icy surface, but his words fell on deaf ears.

We watched as the fastest children filled the coach, which then promptly departed, disappearing into the near pitch-black road. Those left behind looked around uncertainly, unsure if they had missed their only chance and that they would be forgotten or whether they should wait for the coach's return. No one spoke to one another; they only focused on keeping warm and preserving personal space. I looked around at the anxious expressions displayed on their faces.

"They will come back to collect us. Don't worry. They couldn't take all of us at once," I offered, hoping to assuage growing panic. The others seemed to accept my words, and a couple of them even managed a faint smile.

The train began to pull away, billowing bursts of smoke and steam, its departing engine's roar almost deafening. Soon, it vanished from sight, leaving only a faint murmur as it chugged along the tracks into the mountains beyond. The porter lingered on the platform for a while, blowing clouds of smoke as he leaned against his cabin before eventually accepting that we were in no immediate danger and retreating indoors with a loud slam of the door. Everyone turned, fixated on the now-closed door, aware of the warmth on the other side of it. Perhaps a few of us could fit in there and find solace from the bitter cold, but none of us had the courage to knock and ask. Maybe, when desperation had set in, we would summon it.

The conditions grew increasingly harsh, and every passing second felt like an hour as we stood there, shivering. Instinctively, we huddled closer, seeking comfort and warmth from one another. After what seemed like an eternity, one of the boys finally approached the cabin door, his feet crunching on the icy ground. He knocked repeatedly, and we all stood in silence, our eyes fixed on the unfolding scene. The door swung open, revealing the impatient figure of the porter, clearly inconvenienced by the interruption.

"What do you want? Be quick about it, boy. You're letting the warmth escape," the porter grumbled, annoyed. The young boy stood there, transfixed, momentarily preoccupied by the inviting warmth that beckoned from within.

"Please, sir, we need to sit by the fire. Can we come inside?" the boy asked earnestly, his words hanging in the frigid air.

The porter looked at the child, his impatience evident in his posture, before casting a dismissive glance over the huddled group. He reluctantly relented, recognising the urgency of the situation.

"Three of you, and quickly," he responded curtly, his voice carrying enough volume for all of us to hear. With that, he turned away, leaving the boy standing there. The child glanced back at us, a smug grin spreading across his face, before swiftly making his way inside. Two more of our group seized the opportunity and followed suit, disappearing into the warmth. The porter reappeared, slamming the door shut, and scolding the youngsters for leaving it open.

I didn't blame them for seeking warmth, but a pang of jealousy welled up within me. They were quicker than the rest of us, and there were young ones among us who urgently needed the comfort. In that moment, I felt a profound sadness for the children here, with no one to look out for them. No child should ever be left alone to fend for themselves. I missed my father more than ever just then, and I knew he missed me, too.

While we waited, the biting cold penetrated our layers, its icy fingers threatening to sap our strength. We huddled closer together, trying to share warmth, hoping to stave off the chill. Amidst the howling winds, the faint sound of hooves clattering against the stony road reached our ears, carrying with it a glimmer of hope. We turned to one another, smiles lighting up our faces as the monks emerged with the empty coach. We eagerly climbed up a rickety ladder into the coach, wanting to waste no time. With a quick assessment of our group, one of the monks signalled to the one holding the reins, and the horses began their measured movement.

"Wait!" I shouted, springing to my feet. "We forgot the three inside the cabin!" I leapt down the small wooden ladder and sprinted towards the cabin door, knocking insistently. The porter begrudgingly opened the door, a scowl etched across his face, ready to voice his annoyance. But I ignored his words. Instead, my gaze darted beyond him to the three boys, comfortably seated by the roaring fire. I relayed the message that the monks had arrived, and without waiting for their acknowledgement, I swiftly returned to my seat, aware that I had momentarily delayed our escape from the bitter cold. Yet, I knew that I had done the right thing.

Soon after, the wheels of the carriage began to traverse the rugged roads that would lead us to the remote orphanage.

CHAPTER 9

*D*espite the biting cold that seemed to seep into my very bones, exhaustion overcame me, and I managed to drift into a fitful slumber. Weariness from the long journey weighed heavily, causing my eyes to close and my mind to retreat into a dream. In my sleep, I found myself enveloped in the warm embrace of my father, who was kneeling beside me on a sunny fishing trip. But the tranquillity of the dream was short-lived, abruptly shattered by a sharp jolt as the carriage hit a pothole. I awoke with a start, the remnants of the dream fading into a mere whisper. The monks, who had been quiet until now, began to call out, signalling the horses to halt. I looked around, the darkness slowly giving way to the approaching dawn.

As the horses obediently stopped, my eyes fixated on the sight before me—the outline of the monastery emerging from the darkness. It stood as a beautiful, ancient relic preserved by the traditions of its inhabitants. But despite its architectural splendour, the monastery appeared cold and austere, its grey walls devoid of any promise of warmth or comfort. Although I felt disappointed at the bleak surroundings, it was momentarily overshadowed by my father's instruction to locate the portal. Finding it would mean the chance to see my dad again, and I held onto that hope with fervour.

I replayed his instructions in my mind, afraid to forget a single detail. Surveying the grounds as we approached, I searched for the stone wall and the woods beyond it. Though the darkness still veiled the area, I could just about make out the faint outline of the stony perimeter. The woods, according to my father, could be found toward the rear of the orphanage. He had told me about our lineage's unique ability to sense portals and how practising this gift could reveal patterns in nature that guided us to hidden gateways. I scanned my surroundings, hoping to discern any hints or signs. I stared at the silhouettes of the dark trees, attempting to decipher the direction in which their branches pointed.

"What are you doing?" a small voice interrupted my thoughts. I glanced down to find Isabelle looking at me curiously. At that moment, I suddenly felt the urge to confide in her, to share the weight and excitement of my secret. But then I remembered my father's words, emphasising the importance of protecting our hidden world through secrecy. Looking at young Isabelle, I couldn't fathom what harm she could cause, but I remained faithful to the promise I had made to my father.

"Oh, nothing. Just taking in our new surroundings. It's a bit grey, isn't it?" I said, gesturing to the looming rock walls of the orphanage.

Isabelle nodded in agreement, her eyes fixed on the imposing structure. Not wanting to dampen her spirits, I quickly added, "But I'm sure they have a nice, warm fire inside where we can rest. And there must be games for us to play. Maybe even a big room just for games. And a library too, I'm sure. The monks need to teach the children, after all."

Isabelle silently nodded, seeming to be appeased by my words. Deep down, I silently hoped that there would indeed be a games room and a library, anything to bring joy to the apparent bleakness.

"This way!" commanded a monk dressed in grey, standing under a flickering lantern next to a large wooden door. We gathered our bags and descended from the carriage. I could only hope that what I predicted about a warm fire waiting for us inside was actually true.

We navigated the gardens surrounding the front of the orphanage, making our way toward the monk stationed at the door. "Hurry up," he shouted, urging us to quicken our pace. With his command, we entered through the weathered door, and the feeble light from his lantern revealed faint carvings on its wooden surface. Scratched and faded, the markings remained indecipherable to me. Walking past the monk, holding the light, I looked up at him and offered a polite smile. "Thank you, sir," I said, unsure if the words had even escaped my lips, as his face showed no sign of acknowledgement. His stern demeanour reminded me of the Postmaster back in our region, for whom my father had been commissioned to build a new sorting rack.

My encounter with the Postmaster, a most serious and stern man, taught me the importance of respect toward not just our elders but anyone we might serve, which, as my father later explained, could be anyone we encountered. The Postmaster never smiled; he boasted an impressive moustache, meticulously twisted and curled into perfect symmetrical circles at the ends, and I never saw him wearing anything other than his pristine uniform. I remember meeting the Postmaster for the first time when my father took me to see the new sorting shelves he had built for him. While most of my father's customers would pat me on the head and converse politely, asking about my favourite sports or books, the Postmaster never seemed to acknowledge my presence. My father had prepared me for such encounters—I would smile and politely greet him with a "Good morning, sir," which would be met with silence.

As I pondered this memory from what was beginning to feel like a former life, we followed the other children into the dimly lit corridor, our footsteps echoing against the stone floor. "Keep up," a monk ahead called out, and we continued towards the sound of his voice. The smooth stone slabs beneath our feet reflected the dim flickers of candles and lanterns that illuminated our way. I couldn't help but wonder about the age of this place and how long the monks had called it their home. Perhaps a thousand years wouldn't be an exaggeration.

We passed by several large chambers, each featuring a solitary fireplace and a group of children huddled around it, seeking warmth from the crackling flames. Shadows danced along the corridor wall as we made our way, and it struck me how many children occupied each room. Yet, despite the multitude of young souls, an eerie silence pervaded the air. There was no play, no conversation—at least, none that I saw or heard. An uneasiness settled within me, a normal environment for children involves games and laughter. I looked down at Isabelle, silently walking beside me, and realised that if I felt unsettled, she must have felt the same. Leaning down to whisper in her ear, I reassured her.

"I told you there would be a nice, warm fire for us to sit by," I whispered, a faint smile crossing my lips. Isabelle returned the smile, though her eyes held a hint of uncertainty.

A strange atmosphere seemed to hang in the orphanage, preventing us from feeling truly at ease. It was akin to an unpleasant scent that permeated certain places, though I detected this using a different sense altogether. Perhaps it was the same sense my father had tried to teach me to use when locating portals—a sense that allowed one to perceive hidden gateways in the world. I thought about this as we made our way to our rooms, noticing that each child here was merely trying to survive.

Every so often, the group would pause, and a portion of those at the front would be led into a room filled with beds. These rooms were sparse, with rows of beds lining the walls. Many lacked windows, the illumination provided by a scattering of candles. I noticed that not all of them had a fireplace, and I fervently hoped that ours would be one that did.

Finally, we ascended a narrow spiral staircase, the steps seemingly endless in their number. Though I couldn't accurately gauge how many we had climbed, the slow progress made it feel like there had been hundreds. When Isabelle and I eventually reached the summit, we were met with a large, calloused hand which came to rest on my chest. I looked up to find the monk who had been leading us, but his gaze was focused on the children in front of us.

"Okay, you lot, into the room," he commanded, his hand still firmly planted on my chest. With his other hand, he opened a nearby door, which flooded the narrow space with light. It had been dark for so long that I had lost track of time. I realised then that sunrise couldn't be too far off, though it still took me by surprise.

As my eyes adjusted to the light, I watched the others file into the room ahead. They quietly claimed their beds, placing their belongings beside them - if they had any. The room had a few occupants already there, and they sat up in their beds, watching silently as the newcomers joined them. It reminded me of the scene at the train station yesterday, where people observed without remark or acknowledgement. The lack of reaction unsettled me, as I had never experienced such indifference before. Later, I would come to understand that this

43

was due to the atmosphere that permeated this place—a part of a system that operated within its confines. It's difficult to describe, but it seemed to affect everyone who encountered it. In the stories my father would read to me before bedtime, there were often witches and wizards, magical adventures where an evil spell cast over the land would cause victims to fall under its control. A brave knight would eventually break the curse and free the land from its grip. It was somewhat similar in this place, though perhaps without the witches and wizards.

The monk waited until all the children in front of me had entered, leaning inside to verify the numbers. His hand remained on my chest, unyielding. Then, he looked down at Isabelle and me.

"You two, come along. Inside you go," he said, his voice low and firm.

We stepped into the room, and the monk swiftly shut the heavy door behind us. The others had already claimed their beds, and a silence hung in the air, interrupted only by the sound of bags being shuffled. Several faces stared at us while others busied themselves, arranging their belongings. Two beds remained empty in the far corner.

"Hey, Isabelle, I think these are for us. Come on, let's settle in and make this our home for the foreseeable future," I said, carefully placing my belongings under one of the free beds and taking a seat. The mattress was incredibly uncomfortable, its roughness scratching against my skin—no wonder the children here weren't playing and laughing.

Above the beds, a small window framed by painted metal bars caught my attention. Curious, I climbed up to peer outside. The sight before me took my breath away—we seemed to float among the clouds, with towering mountain peaks piercing through the cotton-like blanket. Through breaks in the sea of clouds, I glimpsed vast forests and sprawling farmland far below. It reminded me of the lake where my father had shown me our family's secret gift, a reminder of who I truly was—a prince from another world. I inched higher, attempting to peer down into the grounds below. I caught sight of the gardens, the orchards, and although concealed from the window's view, was what I would later discover to be the field with the stone wall and the woods beyond—the place where the lightning-struck tree and the hidden portal resided.

A gentle tug on my shirt brought me back to the confines of the orphanage. I quickly descended from the window and joined Isabelle on her bed.

"We're high in the mountains here. You can see so far," I said, my words punctuated by a shiver. A cold draft suddenly ran through me, and I wondered how I hadn't noticed it earlier. Isabelle stood on her bed precariously, her hands barely reaching the windowsill. I offered my back as a boost to reach the window.

"Wow, we're above the clouds," she whispered in awe.

I let her marvel at the sight while a new problem took hold of my thoughts—how would I leave her behind so I could explore the grounds on my own and locate the hidden portal? My father had emphasised the importance of having a valid reason for frequent visits. Yet, I couldn't imagine leaving Isabelle alone. I considered her like a little sister, and the idea of abandoning her at any point weighed heavily on me.

A familiar voice called from behind, "Pierre is it?".

As Isabelle was still standing on my back, I replied without turning to look — "Yes, it's me," I said.

Isabelle hopped down and made eye contact with the owner of the familiar voice; I smiled. "Hey, Marc! You're in our room too!" I exclaimed.

"Yes, thankfully. It's great to see a friendly face," Marc

replied, clearly relieved. As we caught up on the rest of our journey since the encounter on the train, a loud bell suddenly began to ring, echoing through the orphanage. We exchanged uncertain glances, unsure of its meaning. Without a word, those who were not a new arrival like ourselves rose from their beds and made their way toward the door.

"Come on, let's follow them. It's probably time for breakfast," Marc suggested, assuring us that the ringing bell likely signalled the start of the morning meal. The three of us joined the resident orphans, and in turn, other evacuees followed as we ventured back into the narrow corridors of the orphanage.

CHAPTER 10

We followed the stream of people, their footsteps echoing through the winding corridors. The walls varied in texture, sometimes rough and rocky, hewn from the mountainside itself, and other times smooth, constructed with large stone bricks or adorned with wooden panelling. As we ascended and descended numerous flights of stairs, my hand trailed along the walls, seeking stability and grounding amidst the disorienting labyrinth. The number of steps of each flight began to blur together, and I found myself losing track of our location within the monastery. It felt as though we were delving further into its depths, the rough rock walls indicating the possibility we were on a subterranean level. But in the dim candlelight, it was impossible to know for sure.

Hungry and eager to explore, I yearned to step outside and satisfy my curiosity about the surrounding area. However, I reminded myself that there would be time for exploration after breakfast. The feelings of anticipation of what lay beyond the monastery's confines mingled with the growling of my empty stomach.

At a corner, the corridor abruptly opened up into a vast room flooded with natural light. The sunlight poured in through large windows on one side, casting a warm glow across the space. Rows of benches filled the room, and children streamed in from various doors, guided by monks who directed them to vacant seats. Each table held stacks of empty bowls and piles of spoons, awaiting the imminent meal.

"I wonder what's on the menu," Marc mused, glancing at me with a playful smile.

"Something tells me it might not be quite what we're used to," I replied with a touch of scepticism. We took our seats, feeling uncertain about the proceedings. Although I had never been here before, the scene felt familiar—a pervasive silence, everyone absorbed in their own thoughts. Just then, a commotion erupted near one of the tall windows on the opposite side of the room, capturing the attention of everyone at our table.

In unison, we turned to face the disturbance. A bowl crashed to the floor, and the sound reverberated through the room as metal collided with the cold stone slabs. Eric, standing threateningly, confronted a few seated children. Their conversation remained indecipherable to me being so far away, but the tension hung palpably in the air. Suddenly, Eric seized one of the boys by the back of his shirt and forcefully threw him to the ground. Marc got up immediately, his protective instincts kicking in.

"Not again," I thought, apprehensive about the brewing confrontation. I tried to reassure and dissuade Marc, understanding that intervening might only escalate the situation. Placing my arm on his shoulder, I attempted to calm him down.

"Marc, sit down. This kid has some problems. Fighting fire with fire isn't going to help him or anyone," I pleaded, hoping to diffuse the rising tension. He angrily shrugged off my hand.

"You don't get it. No one stands up to him. He gets away with it all the time," Marc retorted, his frustration evident. I reflected on the time I first encountered Eric and his younger brother at the train station, where their drunk father had subjected them to harsh words. While I knew that what Marc was saying held some truth, I also knew that Eric had faced his own challenges. The complexity of the situation weighed on my mind.

Before the confrontation could intensify further, a monk materialised out of nowhere, swiftly seizing Eric by the scruff of his neck and carrying him towards one of the doors. Eric put up a fight, kicking and screaming, knocking over a couple of chairs in his struggle. However, his efforts proved futile against the monk's unyielding grip. The monk said nothing, maintaining his composure as he disappeared through the door, taking Eric with him.

"Good," Marc said with a hint of satisfaction. "Hopefully, he'll stop being so selfish." He sat back down, his anger subsiding. However, a pang of sympathy tugged at me, even though Eric and I had crossed paths this way before, and he likely provoked the recent incident. Discipline was obviously necessary, but I couldn't shake the feeling that there was more to Eric's story.

Soon after, the clang of a bowl being struck interrupted my thoughts. In unison, all heads turned towards the sound —a monk standing before us, his gaze sweeping across the room. He lowered his head in a moment of silent prayer, his words spoken in Latin, their meaning lost on me. The rhythmic movement of his hand, tracing the sign of the cross across his forehead and chest, signalled the end of his prayer. Two monks entered, pushing large steaming vats. Hope surged within me as I silently repeated a plea: "Please be porridge."

Some children stood up, forming an orderly queue, picking up bowls and spoons. I looked at Isabelle.

"Come on, let's get some breakfast," I said, standing up next to Marc. We joined the queue, eagerly awaiting our food. As we reached the front, the monk gestured for my bowl. I handed it over, watching as he ladled a scoop of the steaming contents of the vat into it. The mixture was somewhat watery, splashing onto the monk's apron in the process. I peered into my bowl at the grim sight before me. Giving the monk an empty thanks, I returned to our table, cautiously approaching my first spoonful. My first impression was that it wasn't as bad as it looked, but it paled in comparison to the heavenly oats my father used to prepare for me. I glanced at Isabelle, who stared at her untouched food, the spoon neatly resting beside it.

"Are you okay?" I asked, concerned by her solemn expression.

"It looks disgusting," she whispered quietly, with a sad expression on her face. I couldn't deny the unappetising appearance, but I knew that hunger and necessity compelled us to consume it.

"I know," I empathised. "But sometimes, you just have to hold your nose and swallow it quickly." Isabelle's eyes filled with a hint of anger, her disappointment apparent. Worried that my attempt to help might exacerbate her negative feelings, I tried a different approach. "Imagine it's hot cocoa and go for it," I suggested, hoping to make the experience more bearable. She stared back at me, annoyed. Reluctantly, she picked up her spoon, resigned to the limited option before us. There wasn't much choice, and hunger superseded our distaste.

Shortly afterwards, a pair of monks came in, carrying

large baskets filled with bread. They distributed the loaves to each table, and we tore them apart, using the bread to absorb the remaining 'porridge' in our bowls. Some children placed their empty bowls onto large racks at the back of the room, presumably leading to the kitchen. With our empty bowls stacked together, we returned to our seats, uncertain about what would happen next. The unspoken question of how things worked in this place lingered as our inquiries yielded minimal answers from those around us who knew. At least we had grasped the routine of breakfast, though I couldn't help but hope for something different on the menu. Considering the scarcity of resources due to the war, it was likely that bread and watery oats would be it for the foreseeable future.

My gaze shifted towards the tall window, the vibrant blue sky beckoning beyond its frame. Soon, I would have the opportunity to explore the grounds and unravel the mysteries of this monastery. However, my attention was drawn towards a lonely little boy sitting near the base of the window. It was Eric's younger brother, appearing lost and isolated in the bustling room. I glanced at Marc and Isabelle, who were both absorbed in their own observations, taking in the vastness of the room. My heart went out to the little boy, feeling a sense of obligation to offer him some reassurance and friendship. I didn't even yet know his name. Although there wasn't enough space at our table, this seemed like one of those moments when my father's advice about helping those in need came to mind.

Before I could inform Isabelle of my intentions, the monk struck his bowl again, capturing everyone's attention. We shifted our focus to the monk, who surveyed the room before addressing us.

"Last night, many of you arrived at this monastery. With the increased number, there is a greater need for assistance in maintaining operations and being able to house everyone," the monk announced. "As such, each of you will be assigned a job. I will call each table forward and provide instructions for your tasks."

The announcement of assigned jobs didn't come as any surprise to me. I had often helped my father in his work, lending a hand to clean his tools and keep his workshop organised. When our table was called forward, Isabelle hesitantly stepped toward the monk first, and I offered her a little nudge.

"Dormitory duty," the monk said before motioning for her to move on. When it was my turn, I stepped forward, unsure which kind of task I would prefer. However, the decision was quickly made for me as the monk declared, "Fire duty."

I stepped aside, rejoining Isabelle, and contemplated the nature of my new responsibility.

Once all the children had been given their jobs, another monk emerged from behind the first and, speaking brusquely, said, "Dormitory duty, this way." Isabelle looked up at me worriedly, but I assured her everything would be fine and we would see each other again soon. After the assigned group disappeared, a distinctively different monk entered the scene. With a short beard and a ghastly scar cutting across his eye, he exuded an aura of both fierceness and danger. When he turned, I noticed a large cutting axe securely fastened to his back. He looked out across the room, eventually locking eyes with me. Frozen in place, I waited to see which group he would call.

"Fire duty," he declared, a momentary pause hanging in the air as everyone stared. A smile briefly flickered across his face, breaking the intensity of the moment, before he shifted his gaze away from me. I surveyed the room, hoping to spot familiar faces among my fellow fire duty companions.

However, it seemed that none of my friends were joining me. Suppressing my apprehension, I hastened my steps, half-walking, half-running, to keep pace with the monk. I didn't want to get lost or find myself in any trouble, especially with a monk carrying an axe and a scar etched on his face.

"Keep up!" he shouted from ahead in the dimly lit hallway. I quickened my pace, my breath visible in the chilly air. The monk opened a heavy wooden door, and a burst of light flooded the path. "Run along! It's cold out, so be quick," he said before vanishing outside. I followed suit, the icy cold biting against my skin, a stark reminder that we were ill-prepared for an outing.

Minutes later, the monk emerged from the door, urging us to hurry. Determined not to fall behind, I ran outside and along the narrow gravel path, my eyes fixed on the wooden hut with smoke billowing from its chimney. It was my first venture outside since arriving at the monastery, and the freezing cold pricked my senses. The monk opened the hut's door and disappeared within, only to reappear shortly thereafter.

"Hurry!" he called out, disappearing once more.

As I raced along the path, the realisation of my assigned duty settled in. Fire duty—what a perfect reason to explore the monastery's grounds and provide a legitimate excuse for venturing out to see my father. The excitement of exploration overshadowed the fear of being alone, and I embraced the unknown journey that awaited me.

CHAPTER 11

I stepped over the threshold of the hut, and my senses were immediately greeted by a comforting warmth that enveloped the cosy space. The log cabin exuded an inviting ambience, with vibrant blankets cascading over the bannister of a staircase leading to a mezzanine above. A fire roared quietly in a wood stove on one side, casting dancing shadows across the room, while a kettle stood atop it, ready to fulfil hot drink requirements. Dark red and blue rugs sprawled across the floor, with an assortment of chairs which were adorned with the plush skins of various animals. I sensed a hint of smoke in the air, although it was not unwelcoming but oddly inviting. For the first time since leaving my own, this place made me feel at home.

The monk waited patiently near the door for the last child to enter before abruptly shutting it, cutting off the chill from outside. With a deliberate motion, he removed the axe strapped to his back and placed it carefully on a hook on the wall. Gesturing for us to settle on the cosy rugs, he perched himself upon a chair, commanding our undivided attention.

"Listen carefully," he called out, with a commanding yet

gentle tone. We sat in silence, captivated by his presence. "My name is Alix, and I welcome you to the orphanage and to the esteemed task of fire duty." Intrigued by this man who seemed different from the other monks, I silently pondered his origins. None of the other monks had introduced themselves or shared more than necessary commands and directions. Alix seemed to break that mould.

"Fire duty is perhaps the most crucial responsibility of all," Alix continued, his eyes scanning the room, relishing in the captivated audience. "Warmth is a necessity for survival in these mountains; the coming months will bring heavy snowfall and relentless cold. Our duty is to ensure that the fires remain lit and continue to provide warmth to the entire monastery."

Alix's rapport with us was a refreshing contrast to the mostly austere and harsh atmosphere of the monastery.

"Ah, splendid! I have your undivided attention," Alix said, a smile playing on his lips. "Fire duty encompasses various tasks: gathering, cutting, storing, transporting, lighting, and cleaning the fireplaces and chimneys. You will each undertake these responsibilities during your time here... which will be every day, except on a Sunday." Rising from his chair, Alix disappeared through the door without a word. Uncertainty hung in the air as we waited, unsure of what would happen next. Moments later, he returned, his arms laden with logs.

"Ah, excellent! You're all still here. I do tend to frighten people when they first set eyes on me," Alix chuckled to himself, carefully opening the wood stove door and placing two logs onto the fire. The flames eagerly embraced the new fuel, spreading warmth throughout the cabin.

"You will work alongside me during your stay. You will sleep in your dormitories, have meals in the food hall, and attend mass after dinner with everybody else. I find solace in prayer throughout the day, seeking quiet, solitary spots rather than going to the chapel as the other monks prefer. You will be with me during the rest of the time, carrying out your tasks and earning your keep in this marvellous monastery."

I felt excited at the prospect of spending time with Alix. Despite his appearance, he was an intriguing character.

"Ah," Alix exclaimed, "it seems we're missing a few members of our team." He stood and peered through the window next to the door. "Welcome!" he said with enthusiasm as he swung the door open. His warm reception seemed extravagant, bordering on inappropriate in comparison to how we had been received by everyone else at the monastery. I turned my gaze toward the newcomers, and to my surprise, it was Marc and Eric walking side by side. The sight struck me as peculiar. I wondered if they were now assigned to spend time with the enigmatic Alix as a consequence of another scuffle.

"Eric, how delightful to see you again," Alix greeted him, though if I wasn't mistaken, a hint of sarcasm seeped into his words. Nevertheless, there was still genuine warmth in his voice. "And you too, Marc. Thank you for joining us in this important endeavour of fire duty."

I waved at Marc, who appeared angry and mouthed a hello, grateful to have a friend as part of our team. On the other hand, Eric seemed defeated as he silently took his place on the rugs alongside the rest of us.

"It is now approaching half past nine," Alix declared, standing tall. "Soon, you will hear the bells ringing, calling the monks to prayer. I suggest you all return to your dormitories and find warm clothing. Our first task is to collect firewood from the forests and store them in our woodsheds for drying. I have an excellent system in place, as you will soon discover. Now, off you go, my young ones. I must go and pray." Reluctantly, we rose from the rugs, hesitant to leave the comforting warmth of the cabin. As the door swung open, the bitingly cold wind pierced through my clothes, urging me to hurry back quickly to the main monastery. Racing along the gravel path, I stole a glance at the woods beyond the field, where I knew the hidden portal awaited. My next challenge, I realised, was to find a way to be alone to find this portal so that I could see my father. Secrecy would prove challenging in the presence of so many people.

Eventually, I reached the dormitory, though not without taking a few wrong turns along the way. Hastily, I rummaged through my belongings and selected a random assortment of clothing which might help shield me from the outside elements. Stepping out, I nearly collided with Marc, who was rushing in.

"Hey, Pierre, sorry about that," Marc apologised.

"Don't worry, I'm just glad we're on fire duty together. I have a feeling it'll be an adventure. There's so much to explore in this place," I responded optimistically.

"Yeah, I guess so," Marc replied with a hint of pessimism. Remembering his arrival with Eric, I wondered if he was still troubled by what had transpired earlier.

"What happened between you and Eric? Why did you arrive at the cabin later than everyone else?" I inquired, curious to hear his side of the story. Marc looked at me with a mixture of anger and relief.

"Let me tell you, Pierre, that boy has some serious issues," Marc began. He settled onto a nearby bed, eager to recount his encounter with Eric. "When the monk called us forward to assign our tasks, I was assigned fire duty. So, I started following the others, eager to begin. As we left the food hall, I noticed that Eric was lingering, hands in his pockets and whistling as if he was up to no good. I didn't want any trouble, so I hurried past him." He looked away for a moment, his words uncertain. "As I passed him, he extended his foot and tripped me up, the little troublemaker." Marc paused. Curious, I waited eagerly to hear the rest of the story.

"Well...?" I prompted, my eyes fixed on Marc, waiting for the conclusion.

"I punched him," Marc confessed, a glimmer of pride evident in his voice. "But a monk happened to be just around the corner and witnessed me punch him. He grabbed both of us, scolded us, and made us apologise to each other and shake hands." Marc's expression shifted, shame overshadowing the initial pride in his actions.

"Marc, you can't just go around punching people like Eric," I admonished gently. It was futile trying to reason with someone like Eric. "It's like trying to calm down an angry hornet—Good luck with that."

Marc looked at me with frustration. "Pierre, Pierre, Pierre, you don't understand. On the streets, you have to be tough. You can't let someone get away with that kind of thing."

"The streets? What do you mean?" I asked, genuinely perplexed. "I thought you lived in a mansion in Paris. What do you know about being 'on the streets'?"

Marc appeared puzzled for a moment, his brows furrowing before he responded. "Oh, of course. My dad used to share stories about his experiences when he was younger. Anyway, back to what I was saying... The monk didn't see Eric trip me!"

Unsure how to respond, I redirected the conversation back to fire duty. "Come on, let's go and find Alix and explore the outdoors," I suggested. Marc nodded and retrieved his additional layers of clothing, laying them out on his bed. He selected some brand-new thick socks and placed them next to a pair of never-before-worn boots.

"Nice boots, Marc. They look like they've never seen the light of day," I commented, observing his preparations.

"Um, yeah. My parents sent them to me at my uncle's place before I was sent here," Marc responded nonchalantly. Fully dressed and ready, he walked past me. "Come on, let's go and find out what this fire duty is all about."

CHAPTER 12

*S*tahl and his men filled the waiting Ju 52 transport plane. A couple of vacant seats were positioned next to where Emmerich sat, empty for the scientists they would pick up when they reached the small airstrip in northern Italy. He hoped they would divulge some information regarding their experiments with him, or perhaps he would overhear snippets here and there.

The interior of the plane was not designed for comfort but for utility, which is greatly desired for military scenarios to increase effectiveness over cost. Bare metal structures were Stahl's view for the next several hours. He stared at the various details of the metallic shapes in front of him. He felt resentful that he had to sit in situations like this. Boredom entered easily for people like Stahl; their desire for success drove them away from the ability to enjoy simple things. Ordinary folk would find taking a stroll a pleasant way to enjoy a view and meditate on ideas and memories. For Stahl, this was a pointless exercise, a waste of time. His men sat slumped on the small square seats, some sleeping, others staring ahead, considering their mission objectives, others shouting to each other, garnering some form of conversation over the loud engine noises booming and reverberating into the hull.

He grabbed tightly onto the frame of his seat as the plane passed through a series of turbulent weather. In a few short hours, they had arrived at their destination. The aircraft glided down into the mountain tops, carefully navigating the valleys below. An airstrip opened in front of them; it was a rectangular shape cut out from a field below. The plane touched down its wheels with a sharp jolt, followed by a bumpy ride until the plane became stationary.

Next to the grassy airstrip were the two scientists, waiting with their various equipment. The First Lieutenant Baumann commanded the men to collect the equipment and load it into the remaining space on the plane, which wasn't much. During the short stop, the soldiers, pilots and Stahl all had a cigarette break.

Smoke curled up over Stahl's face from the burning cigarette in his hand as he stood watching the two scientists. His eyes observed them the entire time curiously, and after a short while, he walked up to engage with them. He knew he could get more out of them by building rapport. This was something he was accustomed to and had helped him advance despite rarely wanting actually to build a friendship with someone.

"Hello, gents", he called out. "Cigarette?" He opened a pack from his jacket pocket, offering a cigarette to each of the men. They both shook their heads and declined the offer. "Fair enough then." Looking back to the plane and his men loading up the equipment, he continued. "That looks expensive. What type of equipment is it?" The scientists looked at each other unamused until one piped up with a response.

"It's a highly sensitive radio system, sir." Stahl looked at the boxes covered in dials and buttons.

"Sounds very interesting. What does it do?" Stahl responded, trying to get any tidbit he could.

"It's classified, sir, but without going into too much detail, it's a new radio technology that can 'see' things that you and I can't see". Stahl looked to the scientist, disappointed. He knew what radio was and knew that it was about waves in the air that we couldn't see.

"Well, isn't that how radio works? We can see ships at sea and planes in the skies using radio waves, even if I couldn't see through the clouds or water." The scientist nods to him in acknowledgement.

"Yes, of course, you are correct, but if the cloud wasn't there or the sea flat, and you had a good pair of binoculars, you would see the plane or boat, correct?" Stahl nodded slowly as the scientist continued. "This is seeing something that, under those conditions, you still wouldn't see it. Something that is hidden from the naked eye, you could say." Stahl stared at the man for a while, frustrated with his cryptic response, but at least it was something. His superiors informed him that they were developing a weapon that could win the entire war. Stahl nodded despite having many questions. He knew he had to ask them at the right time.

"I see. Well, I have more questions, but let's get you both onto the plane." The scientists nodded, followed Stahl back onto the plane, and found their seats. Now, with everything secure and everyone sat back in their seats, the plane taxied to the end of the field and started racing back along the airstrip, taking off once again into the blue Italian skies.

* * *

THE PLANE FLEW over the mountain range across northern Italy all the way to the French border. The plane descended again, this time in darkening skies as the sun nearly disappeared behind the horizon. As strong winds blew across the mountainous caps, the plane bobbed up and down, like a small raft being tossed about in the ocean waves, causing violent shaking within the aircraft's interior.

Stahl cursed loudly, blaming the pilots for the sudden eruption of turbulence. It lasted a few more minutes as the plane continued its decline until finally landing at a German airbase at the border of France. The scientists quickly unbuckled themselves as the plane parked in a hangar. They began checking the various equipment and ensuring the delicate electronics were intact. Stahl used this opportunity to take a closer look at the internals as the men unscrewed various panels to inspect connections were still in place. He had no idea how the electronic equipment worked but relished the opportunity of being able to see something he wasn't allowed to.

The men exited the plane and made their way to a nearby barrack to prepare for the journey ahead. They were quickly loaded up into a transport truck and carted off toward the border. The sunset views of pink snow and ice-covered mountainsides with dark green forests were spectacular and reverent. Like a virus, the unit crossed into France uninvited and began their infiltration into the beautiful and unspoilt land. The army truck pulled up at the edge of a forest, and the men jumped out. They loaded their own gear and the scientists' equipment onto makeshift carries and disappeared into the thick forest.

Dressed in white camouflage, the soldiers carefully made their way across a valley side, making camp before they were engulfed in darkness. They created foxholes and several pits for fires. The scientists, not used to living off the land, especially in freezing conditions, were given priority treatment with a soldier tasked to provide them with their own fire and temporary shelters. The conditions were brutal, and most soldiers would struggle to survive such harsh conditions. Despite the severity of the icy forest, the elite unit was well-trained and prepared for such situations. They quickly set up the camp and gathered around the various fires to stay warm. They had a supply of rations to keep them fed for a week or so and wouldn't need to hunt or forage for a while.

Johan Baumann was tasked with setting up communications for Stahl and himself to liaise with superiors to keep them posted and receive instructions. They could receive radio signals as they were still close to the mobile units nearby. They would be in the dark once they moved on from this location. He did this with ease, and in a short time, the temporary base was established. The men had a supper of soup, bread and canned meat high in protein and iron, engineered to help them in the field. Shortly after, as dark descended fully, the soldiers rotated a watch and took turns to sleep through the night.

The bright moon emerged from behind cloud cover, and the starry night shone down on the group of men as they slept. This was the same light shining through the window of the orphanage where Pierre and his friends sleep. The same light shone upon Michael, Pierre's father, who desperately missed his young boy. For one, they planned destruction and despair. For the other, a plan of restoration and peace.

* * *

WITH THE SUN RISING, the specialist unit arose with a couple of soldiers sent out to perform scouting operations, ensuring the surrounding area was clear and to survey where they needed to go.

Stahl and Baumann shared coffee whilst discussing the operational details. The current instruction was to proceed further into the region, but the path would not be apparent until the scouts reported their findings. Stahl picked up his binoculars and stared across the valley, scanning the surroundings. Passing them to Baumann, he puffed his pipe and exhaled thick smoke. The radio next to him started buzzing; receiving an incoming call, he quickly picked up the receiver.

"Commanding officer Stahl." He stared ahead as the voice on the other end communicated with him. "Understood." He acknowledged and hung up the phone. He puffed his pipe again and sipped his steaming coffee. He set down his coffee and addressed his second in command. "Baumann, there is a monastery that houses orphans 15 kilometres from here. We have a spy located nearby, we are to take the scientists there as they need to conduct their experiments." He turned to face his deputy. "Johan, this is a top-secret mission. No one can know we are there. Do you understand?" Baumann looked toward Stahl for a while, knowing exactly what he meant. They couldn't have witnesses who might pass on information which could compromise their objectives. He didn't like this part of the war where innocent lives got mixed in with the actions of soldiers. However, he knew that war wasn't a clean sport but a grim affair, and he was a good soldier, and good soldiers do what their superiors tell them to do. He nodded to Stahl in acknowledgement. Stahl turned to face the scientists who were gathered around one of their devices. One of them was winding a crank on the side whilst the other was staring into a small monitor, apparently fascinated with what he saw.

"Come on, Baumann, gather the men. The scouts will be returning shortly." He stood up, leaving his coffee and pipe, and approached the scientists to see what they had discovered. Johan sat there in silence, contemplating his conversation with his superior. He wasn't exactly sure he could go to the full extent of ensuring the secrecy of this mission. Taking the life of an armed opposing soldier in a war is not the same as silencing an unarmed child or a monk by any stretch. He wouldn't need to worry about that decision if he made sure it didn't get to that point. He told himself he would not let it get to that. He could ensure they executed the mission entirely whilst remaining hidden and leaving without a trace. The objectives could still be achieved with no blood spilt. He stood, ready to inform the men of their next set of instructions. Deep down, he knew that blood would be spilt, but he kept those thoughts deep in the recesses of his mind, and he left. Two steaming coffees sat there, now alone, the only witnesses to the unfolding crimes of savage men.

CHAPTER 13

*M*arc and I hurried back to the cosy log cabin located just outside the monastery exterior. Alix, our new mentor of sorts, was perched on a small fence, his axe slung over his back and his hood pulled tightly around his face. A group of children had already gathered, seeking warmth from the bitter cold. As we approached, Alix hopped off his perch and greeted us.

"Ah, good! Everyone is here," Alix exclaimed. "Listen up. We're heading into the woods to collect firewood this morning. Gather your belongings and keep up!" Without wasting a moment, he set off toward the field my father had described —the one with the stony wall perimeter and the woods beyond. My excitement soared, knowing that this was my chance to find the hidden portal. However, a tinge of doubt crept in. I still hadn't figured out a way to be alone, and doubts plagued my mind. What if I couldn't find the portal? What if my father was mistaken about its exact location? I needed practice, but the opportunity hadn't presented itself yet.

Alix paused near a small wooden shed next to the field.

"Everyone, wait here," he instructed. He opened the rickety door, revealing a dim interior with tools hanging on the walls and boxes filled with small bags. "Each of you will need your own toolset. Come and take one, pass them around, and make sure everyone has one." Alix pointed to a group of children and directed them to fetch wheelbarrows, which would be used to transport the gathered wood back to the storage area.

I was handed a small leather satchel containing a set of tools for our firewood duty. Inside were a pair of secateurs for trimming small branches and leaves, a selection of knives, and a spindle of twine. These were our outdoor equipment, which we had to return to Alix at the end of each outdoor session. Memories of assisting my father with his carpentry work flooded my mind. He always emphasised the importance of caring for and tidying his woodworking tools, teaching me how to handle each one safely. Though the tools provided to us now differed from my father's, I was taken aback by Alix's trust in us.

Alix led our group forward, crossing the snow-covered field toward a locked gate in the far corner. The grounds remained layered with thick snow, untouched by melting, as spring was still months away. The snow beneath our feet was not soft and crunchy but hard and icy, making the journey treacherous. While we stumbled and tripped along the uneven path, Alix seemed impervious to the challenging terrain.

Alix opened a massive padlock which secured the metal gate, and swung it open. We entered the woods, and Alix patiently waited for everyone to pass through, before shutting the gate behind us. "Alright, here we are. There are several wooded areas nearby where we can collect wood for our fires," Alix explained, sweeping his arm to encompass the hidden groves that eluded our sight. "We need different types of wood for a fire to grow and sustain. Start with small, dry twigs, progress to slightly larger branches, and end with substantial logs that burn brightly for hours. If you tend to a fire well in its infancy, it will repay you in its maturity. Remember that. Today, we will start such a fire, and you will learn how to create and maintain it. Most of the wood here is cold, damp, and wet—challenging to start a fire without the correct practice. Nevertheless, I will teach you the principles, allowing you to gain confidence when starting fires back at the monastery with our dry wood."

Alix divided us into three groups, each assigned to gather wood of a specific size—twigs, small branches, and larger branches that he would later convert into logs using his axe. I relished the opportunity to explore the woods, eagerly searching for the tree hollowed by a lightning strike—the tree my father said housed the hidden portal.

I was in the group collecting small twigs and decided that the time was as good as any to venture off on my own to locate the portal. Ensuring I had something to contribute when we regrouped, I clutched onto a handful of twigs I had found near me lying on the ground.

As I knelt to pick up another small stick, my heart began racing and began to feel a peculiar sensation inside my chest. It wasn't a conscious realisation but a deep knowing that the portal was calling out to me. Remaining crouched, I surveyed the nearby area, and my eyes locked onto a raised tree root along what appeared to be a path in the snow. I slowly stood and followed the 'path' with my eyes. Perhaps it was a trail carved out by the animals of the forest as it meandered ahead. I started to walk along it, and as I did so, the feeling in my chest increased and increased. It felt like a balloon inflating within, full of an overwhelming sense of joy. It was my body celebrating the closeness of the portal and my true home that the hidden doorway would open to—not that I knew that at the time. I later came to understand this is how my body would react.

The path, if one could call it that, led to a small clearing, and at the centre was the large tree my father told me about, struck by lightning a long time ago. I stood there in awe of the mighty giant, once full of life, now a burnt-out shell. Gentle winds stirred the surrounding foliage, causing tiny ice crystals to fall around me slowly. The noise of the others in the wood was dampened by the thick snow. I stepped forward up to the tree, my feet crunched into the unspoilt snow beneath, and I laid my hands on the bark. I peered inside and could see the whole tree hollowed out and blackened from the strike. It was large enough for me to step inside, which I did, and I stayed there for a while, knowing this was the place where the doorway to my true home lay.

As I placed my hands on the bark, a tingling sensation surged through my fingers as if a small electric current coursed through them. With anticipation, I extended my hands as if receiving a gift and closed my eyes, focusing on the energy pulsating within me. The portal was calling out; its existence echoed through my being. I didn't need to see it with my physical eyes; I knew it was right there, where I stood.

The approach of others interrupted my reverie, prompting me to step away from the tree and join them casually, my arms laden with the small twigs I had collected earlier. We reconvened with Alix, who proceeded to demonstrate how to start a fire using the wood we had gathered. Smoke billowed, stinging our eyes, but it wasn't long before the fire turned to roaring flames. We gathered around, enjoying the pleasant warmth, captivated as he explained the art of fire creation. Glancing back at the once mighty tree, the thought of reuniting with my father filled me with hope.

* * *

WEEKS PASSED, and the daily routine at the monastery became second nature to me. Despite the bone-chilling cold, I relished the opportunity to assist Alix, learning invaluable skills from him. I now knew how to store wood to ensure it would dry quickly, how to clean fireplaces thoroughly, and how to ignite fires effectively. Exploring the nooks and crannies of the monastery to maintain roaring fires had become a familiar and satisfying task. During this time, I had visited the hollowed tree on numerous occasions, but always in the company of others during our wood-gathering outings. Observing Alix as he sought solace in prayer, I considered stealing a moment for myself, just as he did after lunchtime. It seemed like the perfect opportunity to visit my father through the hidden portal.

When the post-lunch break arrived, I made my way across the snowy field. The locked gate prevented me from taking the usual path, so I headed for the small gap in the stone wall instead. With caution, I climbed the broken-off stones, carefully manoeuvring myself into the wooded area. The silence of the empty forest enveloped me, and a sense of anticipation washed over me.

I hastened my steps, eager to reach the tree that held the portal. Upon arriving, I stood before it, gazing at its weathered trunk for a brief moment. Ensuring no one was nearby, I extended my arms, trying to recall the techniques my father had taught me for interacting with the portal. A tingling sensation sparked in my fingertips, and I closed my eyes, focusing on relaxation. I reminded myself this was who I am, and should be as normal as breathing. I opened my eyes, and before me, a shimmering haze emerged between my hands, similar to how air visibly shifts above a flickering flame. Concentrating harder, the haze distorted further until a tiny opening, no bigger than a button, materialised. Gradually, it expanded, growing to the size of an orange.

Through the opening, I gazed into the warm, familiar forest beyond the portal. It was filled with countless trees, their vibrant green leaves swayed in the gentle breeze. Soft grasses and moss carpeted the ground, and birds chirped joyfully on the branches. I carefully surveyed my surroundings, ensuring that no one could see me. Satisfied that my secret was safe, I decided it would be enough practice for the day.

I was delighted that the skill of opening the portal came to me so naturally; I feared I had forgotten it since I hadn't used it for weeks now. Even though I was elated at the experience, I was sad not to see my father there and decided to throw a branch from the wintry landscape through to let him know I had visited. I hoped the branch would look out of place given that it was clearly from a time of winter and not a warm summer. Looking longingly at the beautiful sunny world, I whispered a quick goodbye and closed the portal, revealing the cold, blackened interior of the tree I stood in. Eagerly, I sprinted all the way back to my dormitory, my mind already plotting my next visit.

CHAPTER 14

I continued to visit the portal most days, concealing my trips to the woods by pretending to gather sticks for fire duty. After each visit, I made sure to have a bunch of sticks under my arm as a cover. Practising opening the portal became a daily routine, and peering through the window into my real home brought a longing to explore. I was tempted a few times to climb through, even sticking my hand through to feel the warm air, but my father's strict rule about entering our true home before our time held me back. To leave a sign of my visits, I would throw a branch or drop a few stones into a pile on the other side of the portal. I noticed my father doing the same—he had arranged a neat pile of acorns next to the tree. I wondered when he visited and felt disappointed that I had always missed him.

Another week passed with missed meetings, and I grew frustrated not knowing when my father would come. I attempted to visit at different times of the day, but it was challenging to do so with our busy schedule and fixed routines. A few new acorns would appear each time I went, but I never saw my father dropping them.

After finishing lunch with Isabelle and Marc one day, I sneaked off to the woods as usual. With more discipline, I approached the tree cautiously, not needing to rush and arouse suspicion. I had a couple of branches ready in case someone challenged me. As I neared the tree, I looked around and then set the branches next to me on the ground. Stepping into the tree, I extended my hands slowly, opening the portal. It had become relatively easy with practice, although I still needed to focus to keep it open. Emptying the stones from my pocket, I watched them crash into the forest floor on the other side. I spent a while watching the birds in the sunny forest in the Endless World before closing the portal and sitting on a snow-covered root by the hollowed-out tree.

Suddenly, the sound of a snapping stick behind me made me jump. Someone was approaching from behind the tree. In a hurry, I gathered the branches I had collected earlier and pretended to search for more sticks. Another stick broke underfoot, and I turned slowly to see who was there. My heart skipped a beat as I recognised my father standing there, beaming at me.

"Father!" I called out and ran straight into his arms. He lifted me up and swung me around.

"Hello, Pierre. I've missed you so much." We hugged tightly, not wanting to let go. "It's really good to see you. I'm pleased to see you've been practising and finding the portal." He smiled down at me, and we sat down together. He handed me an apple, and we caught up, sharing stories from the past few weeks. I told him all about the monastery, the monks, and my new friends Isabelle and Marc. I shared stories about Eric, his younger brother, the monks and the enigmatic Alix. I also explained how I had managed to visit the place without raising suspicion. He listened attentively, happy that I had settled in well and made friends.

"That's wonderful, Pierre," he said, but I detected a hint of sadness in his voice.

"Is everything okay, Father?" I asked, sensing his sombre tone.

He looked at me, trying to find the right words to explain the worsening war to his young son. "Well, I'm really glad to see you, but the war has become even darker in the past few weeks. I still have a lot of work to do." He glanced at the ground, and I realised I hadn't considered when this would be over and when we could return to our normal lives. It seemed like the end was nowhere in sight. He looked back at me. "But I can still come and visit you here." He said and rustled my hair. We both grinned and sat together in a comfortable silence, enjoying each other's company.

Now that we had finally met, I explained my routine and the best times for me to visit the portal without raising suspicion. We were able to meet many more times over the next few weeks. Sometimes, we would share an apple, and other times, he would bring a treat like a chocolate bar. I felt incredibly privileged to have these secret meetings with my father. I couldn't help but feel a tinge of sadness for my fellow evacuees who had parents but couldn't see them and an even deeper sorrow for the orphans who had no such kin. I understood the importance of fire duty and how it kept the children and monks safe and warm during the cold winter months. Just as the warmth of a fire could bring comfort, a fatherly hug or a mother's love could keep one's heart aflame. My father and I discussed at length how I could bring that warmth to those around me, especially to those who had never known a doting mother. He offered advice and shared anecdotal stories of people he had encountered and learned from.

Once, I shared a story about breakfast with Marc and Isabelle in the food hall. I had noticed a child from another table quickly snatch a piece of bread as he walked by and hid it up his sleeve. At first, I hesitated, unsure if I should report it to a monk. But over the weeks, I witnessed other children doing the same. It made me wonder how prevalent this behaviour was. I told my father about it, not knowing what to do.

"Well, Pierre, you must remember that these children have never had someone looking out for them," my father explained. "No one to teach them right from wrong, the simple things you take for granted, like brushing your teeth or tying your shoelaces. They've had to fend for themselves." I looked puzzled, and he continued.

"Why would they steal if they have enough food?" I asked, seeking clarification.

"Who said they have enough food for the day?" my father responded, agreeing with my observation. "You see, you've always had enough to eat, never gone without. But for these children, when they see food on a table, they think it might be their last. They hoard it because they worry there won't be any for tomorrow." Suddenly, I saw those children in a different light.

"But stealing is wrong, isn't it? Especially when there's enough food," I questioned, still a bit confused.

"You're absolutely right, Pierre. You and those children are in the same boat, but you don't steal, and you don't go hungry." My father nodded. "Their decisions are influenced by what's going on in their minds. It's called a 'value system'. The system they follow is about looking after oneself before others. It starts in their hearts, and it's all they've ever known because no one lovingly taught them otherwise." I began to understand but was unsure how we could change that.

"What can we do about it? You said we're supposed to be ambassadors, bringing our way of life to these people," I asked, seeking guidance.

My father chuckled. "Pierre, that's easy! In this particular case, the next time you see someone take a piece of bread, go and offer them a piece of yours. Giving someone your bread is an alternative value system at work. It's about putting others before yourself, especially when you don't have much to offer. It's a powerful action." I stared at my father, taking in his words. I still didn't fully grasp the concept, but deep down, I knew he was speaking the truth.

We had many conversations like this, discussing ways to bring the value system of our true home to the people in this place, including my friends at the monastery.

After our exchange, we stood up from our perch, and I gave my father another tight squeeze as we said our good-byes. I watched the portal appear behind him, tall and wide enough for him to walk through easily. I wondered how he could open it so effortlessly, even when he wasn't paying attention. Perhaps one day, I would be able to do the same. I bid him farewell, and he stepped into the Endless World. We waved at each other, and in a flash, the portal vanished, leaving behind a snowy void and the emptiness of the hollowed tree.

I picked up my sticks once again and ran back to the gap in the wall, making my way back to the orphanage.

* * *

HIDDEN up high in the branches of a tree, Marc slowly extricated himself from a prone position behind a large, broad branch. Carefully descending to the trunk, he jumped to the ground and walked in trepidation toward the tree containing the hidden portal, having just witnessed something supernatural. Examining the space where Pierre and his father had once sat, he searched within the tree for the secret doorway he had seen just moments before but found only the cold, hard, darkened surface. Glancing in the direction Pierre had run off to and then back toward the back of the tree, Marc began running deeper into the woods and the forest beyond. He trod carefully, weaving between branches and leaping over icy tree roots that littered his path. For about an hour, he ventured deeper into the mountains until he reached a small wire fence. He slipped underneath it and followed a track for a few minutes until he arrived at a stone bridge. Climbing down the side of the bridge, he settled into the space beneath it. A small stream flowed under the bridge, its icy banks glistening. Marc found a small ledge and then tucked his arms and legs into his jacket to stay warm.

As he sat hidden, the unique sound of a bird whistled loudly nearby. He stood up and mimicked the sound. Shortly after, two men emerged from the undergrowth, joining Marc beneath the bridge. One of them lit a cigarette and offered another to Marc, who accepted and joined them in smoking.

"Well, what do you have?" one of the men gruffly asked. Between coughs, Marc struggled to explain the strange scene he had witnessed. He told the men that he saw something.

"Yes, that's what spies do. They see, and they hear," the man mockingly remarked.

"I saw something unscientific, something unnatural," Marc responded, his voice tinged with frustration. "I saw a man appear from another place, coming through an invisible door. And then he disappeared the same way, through some kind of door. But when I went to investigate, there was nothing there—just a dead old tree."

"Wait, you want to give us some nonsense instead of real intelligence?" the man retorted harshly, clipping Marc around the ear.

"I'm not making it up. It's exactly what I saw," Marc protested, rubbing his stinging ear.

One of the men cupped his hand and whispered something to the other before they both turned to look at Marc.

"Go and find out more, and come back with something more concrete. And if we find out you've been fabricating fairy tales, I'll throw you right into that river," the man said, pointing aggressively toward the river. "Now, run along." He shoved Marc off the ledge. Marc got to his feet, staring at the two men as he did so.

"Don't I get anything?" Marc asked hopefully. The men laughed, and one of them reached into his pockets, pulling out a chocolate bar wrapped in foil. He broke off a piece and tossed it toward the boy. They then disappeared back into the undergrowth. Marc scrambled to find the morsel of chocolate, quickly shoving it into his mouth. Patting himself down, he ran back through the woods toward the orphanage.

CHAPTER 15

*B*ack at the dormitory, I shrugged off my jacket and made my way over to the smouldering remains of a once-crackling fire in our common room. I carefully tended to the embers, coaxing them to life with small branches and twigs. Satisfied, I added a few logs to ensure the fire would provide warmth for the next few hours without needing immediate attention.

Isabelle entered the room, pushing a large cart designated for laundry. Clean bedding and keeping the halls free of dirt were essential aspects of our dormitory duties. The constant trips outside brought in mud, snow, and ice on our boots, necessitating regular mopping of the floors, which required easy access to mops and buckets throughout the monastery.

While fire duty aimed to provide warmth for everyone, dormitory duty focused on cleanliness and comfort in the orphanage. Apart from Alix, the monks may have been distant and cold towards us children, but they ensured our basic needs and dignity were met.

Spotting Isabelle, who stood as tall as her cart, I greeted her with a smile and walked over to say hello. Since it was almost dinner time, I offered to assist her with the remaining rounds. Despite having different duties, we often found ways to help each other, a mutual appreciation we shared.

"You seem more cheerful today, Pierre," Isabelle remarked, looking up at me with a grin. Aware of my changed demeanour, I desperately wanted to confide in her about seeing my father. However, since I was accustomed to keeping information about the portal a secret, I quickly concocted an excuse.

"Ah, I was just chatting with Alix, and he made me laugh as we walked together," I replied, knowing Alix was known to entertain his protegés. We finished Isabelle's chores, unloading the cart's contents into large containers for washing, and then made our way to the food hall as dinner approached. The sound of bells resonated through the halls, signalling everyone to gather for their meal.

Navigating the familiar paths and corridors, we joined the bustling crowd as we entered the cavernous dining area. Finding our usual spots, we settled down along with many others. The hall quickly filled with the aroma of dinner as the monks moved back and forth between the kitchen.

A monk stepped forward and tapped a ladle against a bowl, capturing everyone's attention. Hungry and expectant, the room fell silent.

"Before we commence our meal, I have an announcement to make," the monk began. I shifted in my seat and glanced at Isabelle, who looked up with curiosity. "Today, we bid farewell to our young Clare Muchin. Her parents are relocating and will be taking her back with them."

Murmurs spread through the hall as children whispered their shock and dismay to one another. Our table shared similar expressions. It was the first time since our arrival that someone had left the orphanage, a poignant reminder for those who had no parents or had lost them due to the devastating war. It emphasised that some children were only here temporarily, while others still had parents waiting for them outside. Adoption had become rare during the war, making Clare's departure a significant event.

The monk called for silence as dismayed voices and murmurs escalated across the hall.

"Please be seated and show respect," the monk commanded. Young Clare rose from her seat, attempting to conceal her joy at the prospect of being reunited with her parents.

The announcement stirred strong emotions among the residents of the monastery. As Clare made her way past the tables toward the monk who would escort her, an infectious jealousy in the air manifested in jeers and shoves from the other children.

Next to me, Isabelle suddenly stood up on her chair, clapping her hands loudly. Faces turned, presenting a mixture of disgust, surprise, and puzzlement. Intrigued, I looked at Isabelle, whispering, "What are you doing?"

"Come on!" she shouted, not backing down. Reluctantly, I rose and joined her in applauding Clare. The sea of faces before us shifted from disgust to puzzlement, all except for one—Eric. He locked eyes with me, his anger evident. We held our gaze until I looked away, intimidated by his stare.

Clare's smile returned as the disapproval subsided. She reached the monk, who bowed gently, and they left the room together. The monk with the ladle and spoon uttered a quick prayer in Latin, and dinner proceeded as usual.

Glancing back across the room, I realised Eric was no longer present. Dread seeped into my core; he was not someone I wanted as an enemy, but based on our previous encounters, he likely already despised me to some extent.

"What was that about?" I asked Isabelle, my tone somewhat accusatory.

"Even though I long to see my Mama and Papa, I'm certain my time will come. This was a special moment for Clare, and we should celebrate it with her, especially if it's something we desire most for ourselves," Isabelle replied, her wisdom shining through, reminiscent of my father's teachings. Her words made perfect sense. I stared at Isabelle briefly, marvelling at the insight of such a young girl as we tucked into our dinner.

After the meal, we returned to the dormitory to prepare for bedtime and the impending lights-out. Turning a corner along one of the many hallways, Eric suddenly appeared, blocking our path.

"Hey, you two," he said aggressively. "Are you looking for trouble?" Isabelle shrank behind me, her previous confidence and courage fading.

"No, but I think you might be," I retorted, holding my ground. Eric stepped closer, his face inches from mine, his heavy breath unwelcome.

"You better watch yourself, boy," he warned, shoving his finger into my chest. I noticed spittle forming on the edge of his bottom lip.

"Eric, we were simply happy at Clare being able to reunite with her family," I replied, feeling his anger. Before the confrontation could escalate further, a monk carrying a lantern appeared from behind. Eric's demeanour immediately changed, and he started laughing, patting me on the shoulder.

"Master Eric," the monk called out with a disapproving tone. "Your dormitory is on the other side of the monastery. Off you go." Eric continued chuckling, squeezing my shoulder tightly, his nails digging into my skin. I winced in pain as he released his grip and vanished down the hall. I looked at the monk, grateful for his timely intervention. He maintained his disapproving gaze at Isabelle and me.

"You two as well," he said sternly. "I don't want any trouble in our sacred hallways." He walked away without waiting for our response, leaving us alone in the flickering candlelight.

Concerned, I turned to Isabelle and asked if she was okay. She looked back at me.

"Come on, let's go," she said, determination in her voice. As we made our way back to our room, I cradled my shoulder, massaging it to alleviate the pain.

My father had once taught me that choosing the path of righteousness could put me in harm's way. I realised I had just encountered it for the first time in my life. Unfortunately, my encounters with harm were far from over.

CHAPTER 16

*F*rustrated by the two men's scepticism, Marc was determined to provide the concrete evidence they desired and prove his point. He concealed himself high up in a cold, moss-covered tree, wearing his now slightly worn new boots and extra layers of clothing to shield himself from the icy cold.

The wind howled through the woods, carrying gentle flurries of snow. Marc's back and legs were covered with a thin layer of fresh snow, providing him with additional camouflage. He had diligently observed and studied Pierre's routine over the past few weeks, sensing that something was amiss. Pierre often disappeared on his own, raising Marc's suspicions. Instead of immediately questioning Pierre, Marc decided to leverage his position of ignorance to gather more information.

As footsteps approached, Marc remained motionless, surveying the wintry scene below. Pierre emerged and opened the portal, glancing around before closing it again. He sat on a nearby log, playing with the acorns his father had brought on previous visits. Time dragged on, and Pierre's father did not appear. Marc's body grew stiff from the cold, and he began to shiver. Finally, Pierre got up, dropped the acorns, and ran back to the orphanage. After waiting a few more minutes, Marc cautiously descended from his hiding place and approached the exact spot where Pierre had opened the mysterious doorway. He searched the area, examining the dead tree and the ground, hoping to find a hidden switch or mechanical device. Crouching down, he picked up a couple of acorns that Pierre had dropped. As he did so, the ground trembled slightly. In a panic, he quickly dove behind the tree, seeking cover. The secret door suddenly opened a few meters in front of him, and Pierre's father stepped out.

"Late again, sorry, son," Pierre's father muttered to himself. He placed a fresh pile of acorns and disappeared back through the portal.

Once the coast was clear, Marc cautiously rose from his hiding place and approached the new pile of acorns. He took a couple and held them up to his eye, examining them closely. A sudden realisation washed over him, and he grinned. Carefully, he placed the acorns into his jacket pocket and raced off toward the stone bridge a few kilometres away.

Marc produced the secret bird whistle, and moments later, the two soldiers in camouflage appeared before him.

"There you go," Marc said, smirking as he handed over the contents of his pocket—a collection of bright green acorns. One of the men took them and examined them intently.

"What's this?" the prominent soldier asked incredulously. "We asked you for proof of your claims, and this is what you bring us?" He handed the acorns to the other soldier and spat on the ground. He reached for his side, unbuckling the pistol holstered there and pointed the Luger at Marc. Marc's face turned white, fearing for his life. But they didn't see what Marc saw.

"Wait! Wait!" Marc shouted. "Look, they're bright green acorns." The soldier holding the gun grunted in frustration, tightening his grip on the weapon. "Wait!" Marc protested again. "Green acorns appear in the summertime, and that was several months ago. I brought you these because these that you hold in your hand are from the place beyond the magical door. You see, it's not possible for them to come from here." The soldier loosened his grip and held out his hand to the other soldier, who was now looking at one of the acorns with interest. He saw his colleague's outstretched hand and quickly placed the acorns into his palm. The soldier holding the gun inspected an acorn, intrigued but not yet convinced. He looked back at Marc.

"Where did you get this?" he asked.

"I told you, it came from the magical door. The boy's father, who visits through the hidden doorway, comes from another world," Marc explained, relief flooding over him as the soldier no longer aimed the gun at him. "He always brings a handful of these acorns and leaves them in piles, I'm assuming, as a sign that he has been here." The soldiers looked at each other, then down at the acorns, weighing and contemplating Marc's words.

The soldier holstered his weapon and reached into his pocket, pulling out a chocolate bar that he tossed to Marc.

"I'm keeping these," the soldier declared, gesturing to the acorns he held. Marc nodded, concealing his chocolate reward, and both parties went their separate ways, leaving the quiet space under the bridge.

STAHL'S IMPATIENCE was well known by his unit and they made sure not to keep him waiting. As the two soldiers hurried back to their encampment to relay their message to their superiors, they understood the urgency. Upon arrival, they headed straight for Captain Stahl and First Lieutenant Baumann, climbing into their foxhole—an expanded space that now resembled a makeshift camp, complete with a table, chairs, and a mesh roof covered in snowy leaves and twigs. Stahl sat next to Baumann by the table, puffing on his pipe, while the two scientists worked behind them, engrossed in their experiments and equipment.

Seeing their men return, Stahl stood to signal his readiness to receive their message.

"Sir, we have important information," the soldier spoke promptly, knowing not to dither. "The spy staying at the orphanage made contact with us and claims to have witnessed something that initially seemed ludicrous but now holds weight." The two scientists behind the men stand up, highly intrigued by the conversation. Annoyed by the scientists' presence and their tendency to overstep their bounds, Stahl shifted on his feet. The soldiers reported to him and not to anyone else.

"Continue," Stahl commanded, ignoring the scientists.

The soldier held out his hand, displaying the contents. "He handed us these." Stahl took the objects—acorns—and examined them with bemusement. He looked at his men for an explanation. The scientists crowded around Stahl to peer at the small objects.

"What are these?" Stahl asked impatiently.

"Notice the colour, sir," the soldier explained. "They appear fresh, like they've just fallen or been plucked from the trees. But the time for that passed several months ago. This boy claims to have seen another world through a door and a man stepping through it. He insists that these acorns are from that other world—a world in the midst of summer." Intrigued, Stahl commanded his men to move out and head to the orphanage at first light. He turned to the scientists, who were hovering like pet dogs, and handed them the acorns as if they were treats. Excitedly, the scientists began inspecting the acorns, launching into new experiments. Stahl watched them for a while, amused by their enthusiasm. Perhaps this discovery could be a crucial turning point in the war. He inhaled from his pipe, settling back into his chair while his subordinates busied themselves with preparations for the next phase of their operation.

The German special forces unit rose early the following day and set out for the monastery. They easily navigated the mountainous terrain, reaching the woods leading to the portal and the orphanage within a few hours. The forest was enveloped in valley fog, adding to the air of mystery surrounding their mission.

Baumann, realising the importance of secrecy, raised his hand abruptly, signalling the men to stop and crouch down. He crawled over to Stahl, determined to convey his concerns.

"What is it?" Stahl asked, impatiently.

"Sir, the spy informed us that the device is located in the woods up ahead," Baumann explained, trying to sound confident. "I suggest we set up a watch nearby to observe the tree where the device is hidden. Once the area is clear, the scientists can conduct their experiments discreetly—"

"Baumann, get to the point!" Stahl interrupted, frustrated.

"I believe it would be wise to observe before making our presence known. If we engage with the monastery directly, word will spread, even if we take the monks captive and secure the area. The nearby villages will sense that something is amiss." Stahl glared at Baumann, displeased by the interruption, but recognising the validity of his advice.

Keeping the mission covert was paramount, and a cleaner approach was preferable.

"Fine," Stahl agreed.

Baumann returned to his men and relayed the new plan. They found a suitable vantage point and set up camp, positioning two soldiers on the watch to observe the tree and its surroundings.

The first lieutenant settled into his newly dug foxhole, filling his pipe with tobacco and lighting it. He puffed on it steadily, fixing his gaze straight ahead. Another narrative fought for his attention: the possibility of failure and the inevitable confrontation with the monastery's occupants. Silencing anyone who posed a threat to the mission's secrecy seemed inevitable. Baumann pushed those thoughts aside, focusing on the task at hand.

In the distance, the faint sound of bells echoed through the air. Baumann maintained his stare, smoke from his pipe mingling with the fog, determined to ignore the distant monastery.

CHAPTER 17

*A*fter breakfast, Marc and I made our way over to Alix's wood cabin to begin our fire duty. We carefully crossed the icy paths leading to the familiar wooden hut that belonged to the monk. As we entered, the warmth from Alix's burning stove embraced us. We settled down on the soft rugs scattered across the floor, joining the others who were eagerly awaiting instructions for the day.

A few moments later, Alix stepped into the cabin, stomping his feet on the veranda outside to shake off the excess snow and ice from his boots. "Good morning, everybody!" he exclaimed, clearly delighted to see us. Taking his usual seat, he began to outline the tasks for the day and assign them to each of us. Marc and I were tasked with collecting logs from the wood to replenish the stores for next winter.

As we were about to leave the cabin, Alix called out to us. "Young Pierre and young Marc, can you stay behind? I would like to join you today in the woods." We exchanged grins, unable to contain our excitement. Alix often chose individuals or groups for special lessons during fire duty, and we cherished these rare moments of tutelage. Stepping aside, we let the others exit. Eric, the troublemaker, lingered a bit and taunted us before leaving.

Ignoring Eric's remarks, Alix placed a hand on Marc's shoulder. "Come on, let's gather wood together," he said gently. It struck me as odd that he didn't confront Eric or Marc directly, allowing the situation to diffuse itself. We headed out into the cold morning, the clear sky casting a beautiful glow on the hardened ground, which was once melted snow but now frozen again. We focused on making careful footsteps along the path that led to the wood, avoiding the hazard of looking up.

Inside the shelter of the woods, we began collecting logs, choosing the larger ones. Alix would later use his axe to split them into appropriately sized pieces for the fireplaces. After a short while, he called us together. "Let's sit," he invited, gesturing for us to join him. Alix arranged some dry kindling and skilfully ignited a small fire. As he nurtured the flames, adding sticks and larger logs, it grew into a roaring fire.

I relished Alix's lessons and wondered what he had in store for Marc and me that day. I also pondered why he had chosen us. "Consider this fire, young gents," he began. "It roars well, but soon the dry wood will run out, and our wet logs will eventually extinguish the fire." Uncertain, we looked at the fire, nodding in agreement. "The challenge we face is bringing these wet and even icy logs to the fire and keeping it roaring and hot. Any guesses on how we do this?" Alix continued, expecting one of us to respond with an obvious answer. I stared intently, trying to figure it out.

"You can't? That's why we store the wood and let it dry for several months before using it in the dormitories," Marc ventured, hoping his guess was correct.

"Great observation, Marc," Alix praised. "Indeed, we strategically store the wood to ensure it dries. However, it is possible to use wet logs. Let me explain." Filled with anticipation, we sat there, enjoying the warmth and the impending lesson. Alix picked up a damp log covered in snow and ice. He used his axe to remove the hardened ice carefully. "First, we remove the excess ice and then place the log carefully on top of our fire."

"But wouldn't that put out the fire? You said wet wood would extinguish it," I interjected.

"Another great observation, Pierre!" Alix exclaimed, "It depends on how much wet wood you add. The fire we have now is much stronger than the log I've placed on top. Yes, it will hiss and create steam and smoke, but the heart from the flames will eventually dry the log out. The trick is to keep the fire strong underneath." He added a dry stick beneath the wet log, repeating the process a few times until the log stopped hissing and caught fire. To demonstrate further, he added another wet log. "Eventually, the fire will become so strong that you can use wet logs as if they were dry. You just need to be careful not to overwhelm it."

As we watched the flames dance, I pondered the lesson Alix was trying to teach us. I noticed that he often used fire duty as a metaphor to convey more profound messages. After a while, Alix broke the silence. "Sometimes, you encounter people who are a bit like these cold logs. They seem damp and have icy exteriors. However, if the force of the fire is greater, by persistently engaging with them, the ice melts away." He stood up, signalling the end of his lesson. We followed suit, gathering the wood we had collected and making our way to store it for next year's supply.

* * *

HEADING BACK TO OUR DORMITORY, we walked past the shed that housed the fire duty equipment. I noticed Eric and his younger brother hovering nearby. Anticipating an unpleasant encounter, I glanced at Marc, hoping to navigate the situation differently this time. Remembering Alix's lesson, I regarded Eric as the icy log and decided to be the flame instead.

"Hey, Eric, Alix partners with all of us from time to time. I've seen him work with you before, too," I said, reminding him that we were all treated equally. Eric stared back, his mocking look replaced with disdain.

"You're kidding, right? He clearly adores you two," Eric retorted. "Anyway, I don't care. I wouldn't want to spend time alone with a weird monk."

"It's not true," I countered. Sensing Marc's readiness to intervene, I swiftly changed my approach. I turned to Eric's brother, standing there cloaked in the fear of his brother. I still didn't know his name. "You know, I still don't know your name. What can I call you?" I asked, surprising him with my directness. Eric stepped between us, his tone becoming threatening.

"Did I give you permission to speak to my brother?" he growled. Before Marc or I could respond, Eric's brother spoke up, stepping to the side of his brother.

"My name is Thomas," he said, his voice surprisingly steady. "My friends can call me Tom."

"Hi, Tom," I greeted warmly. "Good to know your name. Come on, Marc, let's go." I gestured to Marc, impressed by Thomas' newfound confidence, understanding that this small act must have been a significant step for him. We hurriedly walked past Eric, expecting a shove that never came. I glanced back, half-expecting Eric to berate his brother for speaking out of turn, but there was no interaction between them.

Thankfully, we reached the dormitory unscathed. Isabelle

sat on her bed, engrossed in a game with her toy bear. Before I approached her, Marc grabbed my arm.

"Pierre, I always rejected your approach to dealing with Eric, but today, it went differently. I'm sorry I didn't listen to you before," Marc said, smiling genuinely.

"It's okay," I replied. "I thought I was going to get attacked by him one way or another, so I was surprised, too." Marc nodded, returning to his bunk. I watched him for a moment, contemplating the change in his attitude. Had he been the log I had applied the flame to?

Walking over to Isabelle's bed, I interrupted her game. "Isabelle, I found out Eric's brother's name," I said, hoping to engage her in conversation. She looked at me with annoyance.

"Tom, yeah, I know. I found out ages ago," she replied dismissively, returning to her game. Slightly deflated, I sat beside her and began recounting the day's events.

For the first time, I realised that we were starting to find some joy in staying at the orphanage. Of course, it would have been far better not to be there at all, but that day had been a good one for some of us.

Despite the new life we were building, circumstances were about to change once again in a significant way. A dark storm loomed on the horizon, threatening everything in its path. The monks had lived and worked in this remote, hidden refuge high in the mountains for centuries. However, the storm would arrive in just a few short days, bringing destruction and upheaval in its wake.

CHAPTER 18

*P*ierre's father, Michael, galloped on his horse, his heart racing, desperately trying to make up for lost time. The increasing responsibility of repelling the invading German forces had been entrusted to him, and he knew that their efforts were becoming futile. Despite the overwhelming presence of evil, Michael held onto the belief that goodness could always be found within humanity, even in the darkest of places.

He rode several miles to reach the forest where he was supposed to meet Pierre. Horseback was his only means of transportation since cars and aeroplanes were non-existent in this mystical world. There were some folk who had the ability to fly, though these secrets remained untold.

As he followed the meandering river along the forest's edge, the colourful trees on the opposite bank shimmered and reflected in the water. The warm air rushed against Michael's face as he spurred his horse on. Finally, he arrived at the designated portal location. Dismounting from his steed, he swiftly changed into his winter clothing, which he had carried in a bag. Before opening the portal, he collected several green acorns, a gift for Pierre. Peering through the small opening to ensure the coast was clear, he then widened the portal and stepped through.

To his disappointment, Michael found himself alone. Frustration overwhelmed him as he kicked a stick on the ground. Once again, he had missed his rendezvous with Pierre. Seating himself on the forest floor, he picked up a piece of wood and took a knife out from inside his pocket. The gentle sound of the blade against the wood soothed him as he began carving.

Unbeknownst to Michael, a man with binoculars watched his every move from a distance. After observing him for a while, the man passed the binoculars to his colleague. The man then raised his rifle and peered through its scope. They remained silent, watching intently as Michael diligently worked on his carvings.

Finally, Michael finished his creation—a beautifully carved stag. He carefully concealed it among the icy leaves, smiling at the thought of Pierre's delight upon receiving it. Woodworking had been his passion since childhood, ever since he was gifted a penknife one birthday. Satisfied with his work, Michael stood and turned towards the tree, ready to resume his own missions.

Suddenly, the bark on the tree in front of him exploded with a loud crack, showering the air with splinters. Shocked and disoriented, Michael stumbled forward, clutching his side in pain. He glanced at his hand, which was now smeared with warm red blood. Realising he had been shot, he quickly opened the portal and stumbled through. Another shot rang out, hitting a tree in the Endless World, causing his horse to bolt and disappear. The portal closed behind him, leaving Michael alone on the other side, his breaths heavy and laboured. He staggered and fell, propping himself against a tree. Glancing towards the distant river, he knew help was far away, but he had no choice but to begin his journey towards it.

* * *

BAUMANN'S ANGER flared as he rushed to the two men keeping watch, drawn by the crack of gunfire. He wrestled the rifle from one of the soldiers, his voice dripping with disgust. "You blithering idiot! You were under strict orders not to engage." The soldier looked back, attempting to justify his actions.

"Sir, a man appeared out of nowhere, and I assumed he was the enemy, so I shot him to prevent his escape." The first lieutenant glared at the soldier, his outrage palpable. With a swift motion, Baumann slapped the soldier across the face. He then turned and barked orders to his unit to secure the area.

Calmly, Stahl approached Baumann, a hint of amusement on his face. "Johan, whatever is the matter? No need to lose your composure over something so trivial. We've proven the location of this secret weapon. We were always going to use the monastery as a base. I entertained your ideas of with-holding our advance, but this outcome was inevitable," Stahl chided.

"Sir, there was no need to shoot the man," Johan retorted, his tone filled with annoyance. "He managed to escape through that magic door. What if there's an army on the other side?" He pushed past Stahl and joined the rest of the unit, working to secure the woods.

"An army of fairies?" Stahl jestingly responded. "It's not ideal, but nothing we can't handle." He called out to the two scientists who were always nearby. "You two, come here." In a few quick steps, they stood before Stahl. "You now have complete freedom to conduct your experimentations. We'll assign a few soldiers to guard the hidden door in case someone else comes through. Remember, report directly to me once you've managed to open that door. Don't go to anyone else." The scientists gleefully retrieved their equipment and began exploring the tree, taking samples of its bark. Stahl glared at them, engrossed in their work and seemingly oblivious to his presence. Another crack of gunfire rang out, interrupting the scene.

One of the soldiers came running back to Stahl, stopping and standing at attention. "Sir, we found a monk hiding in the woods. He attempted to flee, and we gave chase. We shot him, and he's currently receiving medical treatment in the field."

"Take me to him," Stahl commanded, and they left together, joining the rest of the unit that had formed a defensive position, now wary of hidden adversaries.

They reached the field where Baumann knelt over the injured monk, applying pressure to his wound while attempting to extract information. Stahl knelt down, his face level with the monks.

"You shouldn't have run, you know?" Stahl held the injured man's chin, studying his wound. "You startled my men and got yourself shot, you silly fool." He reached for a handkerchief and wiped the red spots off his boot. The monk began chuckling weakly.

"I apologise for that," he managed to say before coughing violently, blood spraying onto Stahl's hand. The German Captain's anger flared in disgust, but he composed himself and continued questioning.

"How many monks and children are at the monastery?" Stahl asked, his tone serious, all traces of false joviality gone. The monk lifted his head, looking Stahl in the eyes.

"Monks?" the monk repeated, turning his gaze to the

German captain. But before he could provide further answers, a fit of coughing overcame him.

Stahl stood up, his face twisting with anger. He grabbed the monk's cloak and forced him to stand, pointing towards the ancient monastery carved within the mountainside. "Look at that ancient monastery," he growled. "That's mine now."

"Thank you for allowing me to see my home one last time," the monk whispered before his body went limp. The monk's body collapsed, devoid of the strength to stand or even crouch. He lay on the cold ground, staring up at the blue sky, his lips moving in prayer.

"Dear Lord, thank you for granting me the privilege to serve you at the wonderful orphanage and the friendships I forged. I pray for their safety on their journey ahead, and may their fires burn brightly, warming those around them. Amen." He lay perfectly still, at peace. He kept staring up at the sky even though his spirit left him.

CHAPTER 19

*D*igging into the icy hard ground was laborious work. The shovel barely produced more than small clumps of ground with each strike. It was more akin to digging into concrete. First Lieutenant Baumann knew the darker sides of war all too well and had unfortunately witnessed enough to know how messy it could get. This was one of those scenarios. He accepted that the monk had to be shot for not surrendering, but he still deserved basic dignity. Baumann rested from the arduous work and looked to his superior, Stahl, who was surveying the monastery on the far side of the field.

A hatred for Stahl grew in Baumann's heart. The cruelty and indifference over an innocent life disturbed Baumann's internal fortifications as his humanity mounted an attack.

With the grave dug, he gently lowered the monk into it. Placing the axe on the monk's chest, Baumann closed the man's blue eyes. Despite his brutal end, the monk appeared peaceful to the lieutenant.

Regretfully picking up the small shovel, Baumann began

to fill in the hole with the mounds of icy dirt surrounding the grave.

Stahl returned to Baumann and the rest of his elite squad. He commanded his men to capture the mountainside monastery and secure the area. Baumann stood, hovering by the fresh mound where Alix lay, torn between duty and compassion. He looked to his men, following his superior, Stahl.

"Damn you," he whispered quietly, then turned to join the unit as they crossed the snowy field and entered the orphanage grounds.

* * *

THE SUN STREAMED into our dormitory, highlighting specks of dust floating peacefully through the air. I sat with Isabelle and Marc, discussing how we could get Eric's younger brother, Tom, to spend time with us away from his brother.

"Perhaps, Pierre, you could ask Eric to help you collect wood or something," Isabelle suggested, her plan laid out. I glared at her, a hint of disagreement in my expression. In response to my look, she went on to explain her rationale: "Marc doesn't quite have the same calmness when it comes to Eric... So, he can be the one who asks Tom to help him instead. Then, when your duty is nearing the end, Marc, you can finish early and then come straight here, bringing Tom with you." I looked at Marc, who grinned and nodded his approval at the idea.

"You expect me to keep Eric occupied and content for longer than five minutes? You must be joking, right?" I scoffed at Isabelle, who was now standing carefully on a crate to peer outside.

"Yes, exactly," Isabelle responded without looking back at me. "Eric might surprise you."

The bells started to ring, signalling breakfast time. Marc stood up. "Come on," he said. "You've got your big assignment." He laughed as we got up from the bed, pointing at me as we approached the door.

"He might surprise me by not insulting me, I guess," I said as I turned to Isabelle, responding to her earlier comment, but she still hadn't left the window. "Isabelle!" I called out. "Come on, let's go." She turned around slowly, tears streaming down her face, fear etched into every feature. "Isabelle?" I called out again, softly this time, taken aback by her sudden sadness.

"S-s-soldiers," she whispered between sobs. I looked at her in disbelief. Soldiers? Immediately climbing up to the window, I looked outside for myself. Down below, scenes of chaos unfolded as I watched soldiers aggressively kicking open doors and pointing guns at the monks and children they had rounded up.

Soon, screams echoed through the hallways, intermingling with the shouts of men. The commanding voices carried a distinctive German accent. The Nazis were here? How? Our perceived net of safety, our refuge in the mountains, was suddenly being torn away from us.

The bells began ringing out again, this time without stopping, drowning out the commotion.

I looked toward Marc, who was still standing in the doorway, peering down the hall. He seemed to show no signs of panic or distress.

"Marc!" I snapped, bringing him out of his melancholy. He ran back to us. "What shall we do?" I asked my friends. Isabelle, still distressed, failed to respond. Marc looked at us calmly.

"There's not a lot we can do. Our best bet is to join the others and see what they want. We're all orphans staying with monks; they aren't going to hurt us," he replied.

"Evacuees and orphans," I corrected him.

"What?"

"We're evacuees as well as orphans, right?" I explained. He stared back at me for a moment.

"Same difference," he replied. He was right. There wasn't really anywhere to go. We couldn't hide without being found eventually. There was nowhere we could go outside of the monastery, especially in the bitter cold. The village the monks travelled to and from might be an option, but none of us knew how to get there. When we arrived by train, it was the dead of night, and we didn't see the route. I looked at Marc and nodded in resignation.

"Let's wrap up warm and take extra items for the others. I doubt anyone was prepared for what's happening," I instructed. With our many layers, we headed out into the hallway, reluctantly making our way toward the commotion outside. Fear gripped each of our footfalls, feeling a desperate urge to run away but knowing there was nowhere to escape to. We were trapped.

Suddenly, a soldier smashed through a door in front of us, brandishing his rifle. As we stood in surprise and fear, he roughly grabbed the back of my jacket and shoved us through the door he had just burst through.

We tried to comply as best we could, but it didn't make any difference. The man continued to be aggressive as he dragged us along with him. We arrived at the food hall, where another soldier was standing at the entrance. We were pushed inside and fell onto the cold stone floor. The door slammed shut behind us, and we looked around. The room was filling quickly. A handful of soldiers herded cowering monks and children into neat rows. One soldier stood out from the rest, sitting on a bench nonchalantly. He smoked a pipe and played with a pistol, seemingly unaware of the chaos around him. He was dressed in all black and had a clean-shaven face and neatly styled hair. He was likely the man in charge.

Fear gripped the entire room as the monks and children sat, careful not to move or draw attention to themselves.

I spotted Eric and his brother Tom sitting together at the end of one of the rows. They, too, remained perfectly still.

As we sat down and took our places, I recalled a lesson my father had once taught me. I had been particularly difficult that day, refusing to tidy up his workshop after I had made a mess. I couldn't remember why I had been so stubborn. I do remember him sitting me down and giving me a number of options. One option was to keep refusing, which would result in punishment and being banned from playing in the workshop. The second option was to tidy up my mess and be allowed future playtimes in his workshop. He explained to me that true obedience comes from choice. In the Endless World, coercion and force were forbidden, whilst choice, freedom, and responsibility were encouraged. He said this rule was the key difference between a good king and a tyrant.

CHAPTER 20

*L*ooking at the faces of the children and monks being brought in gave Stahl a particular delight. He peered occasionally at his men roughly bringing the captives into the large hall and watched them sit. Perhaps some of these children could be used as soldiers, a spoil of some sort.

Stahl held his Luger as he pondered these thoughts. He inspected it, shifting it between his hands. He detached the box magazine and counted eight clean cartridges stacked within. Reinserting the clip back into the hand grip, he mentally reviewed the available ammunition of his unit. They had brought several hundred rounds, various grenades and other such weaponry, as well as rations, the men themselves, the scientists, and their equipment. They didn't have a lot of ammo if they needed to start using it. And this mission was operating under the highest level of secrecy; getting further equipment and supplies delivered would be next to impossible. Stahl surveyed the room, roughly counting the heads in front of him. Using the ammunition would be a last resort, he mused. He knew he had the compliance he needed;

he now needed to maintain it and allow the monks to continue their supply trips to prevent any suspicion from being roused by the locals. He pondered that problem for a short while until his first lieutenant entered the large hall and walked up to him.

Baumann leaned over, cupping his hands and whispered into Stahl's ear. "Sir, that is everyone; the grounds are secure. A monk told me that no one comes up here, especially in the winter months. Regardless, I've set two scouts to watch the lane leading up here to monitor for any visitors."

"Good," Stahl responded. "Go and take a seat. I need to address our new friends." He smiled toward Baumann as he dismissed him. He knew he had to occasionally reward Baumann to keep him behaving well, like you would with a dog.

Stahl stood carefully, peering into the faces of those at the orphanage. In that moment, Stahl experienced sheer delight in his corrupted heart as he held the gaze of his audience. He took immense pleasure from the scared faces before him, feeling god-like in that moment.

"I present to you all a deal," his voice booming across the hall, projecting his newly asserted authority over the former hosts. "My men and I need to make use of this..." He paused, searching for the right word from his environment, "monastery," he resumed. "You will continue whatever it is you do here. There is, however, one stipulation that you must adhere to and respect. No one will be allowed to leave the grounds under any circumstance. And in return, I will, in my good graces, let you live." He looked about at his terrified audience, relishing each moment like a young child would with a sweet dessert. "It seems like a fair deal to me," he continued. "And before you know it, we'll be out of your hair." He said jovially. "My first lieutenant, Baumann, will look after you, and I look forward to working with you peacefully." He said the last bit with an air of a threat. The message was soundly received by the discerning monks. Baumann started to make his way toward Stahl as his captain jumped off the bench and headed toward one of the many exits. He nodded to Baumann as he walked past and left the great food hall.

* * *

ISABELLE GRIPPED my hand tightly as the man dressed in black walked past and out of the room. I looked around, searching for Alix. Deep dread washed over me as I couldn't spot him amongst the monks present. I turned to Marc.

"Can you see Alix?" I asked, and Marc scanned the room as well.

"No. I'm sure he's fine, though," he responded. I looked at him, dried tears leaving trails down his cheeks.

"I hope so. It will be alright. Like you said, we should be fine as long as we do what we're told," I tried to reassure him.

Still failing to locate Alix, I wondered where he could be. I could see all the other monks, but he was the only one missing. Perhaps he had managed to hide, or he could be in the woods, unaware of the situation. I hoped he would spot the danger and stay clear, seeking help. Despite my best efforts to reassure myself, tears welled up involuntarily, flowing silently down the sides of my face. I went into a sort of shock as the first lieutenant started to speak. His words washed over me as I realised the reality of the danger we were in.

The German soldier stopped addressing us. Row by row, we were given some bread and then were able to leave the room under instruction to continue our regular routines and duties. I followed the others, numb to the recent turn of events. Isabelle was still gripping my hand. I looked down at her, and she looked up, smiling at me. Her expression shook me out of my trance.

"We can still fulfil our plan with Tom and Eric," she said gently.

"Sorry?" I replied, still in shock.

"It sounds like life will carry on as it has been the past few weeks. You might not be allowed to go to the woods as much. I say we carry on with our plan to spend time with Tom." She looked surprisingly optimistic.

"Weren't you present in the room just now?" I asked, bewildered. I had to bite my lip to prevent myself from bringing up the fact that we were being held captive by dangerous men. I knew it would scare her. She was just trying to help. The smile faded from her face. "Sorry, Isabelle. I'm just struggling to see how we can carry on like before. We are prisoners right now."

"It's okay. Let's just give it a go."

"Sure," I conceded, without any real intention to carry out the plan.

As we walked, a different plan started to form within me. A distraction from the current situation, a glimmer of hope in the darkness. Like a virus multiplying, it began to take over my thoughts: We could escape. We could use the portal to escape from here. All we had to do was go out to the woods, and in a flash, we would enter the Endless World. The warnings from my father around secrecy seemed negligible now; we were all in serious danger, and this way promised safety. He had reminded me multiple times not to enter the Endless World before my time, but he had been going there regularly in order to visit me, deeming it necessary given the extenuating circumstances. So I guessed that, in certain situations, it was permitted. I wasn't sure, but I couldn't see any alternative solution. It was settled in my mind. The problem now, albeit a big one, was going to be getting to the woods. With the roaming soldiers, it seemed impossible. The German dressed in black had made it clear— we must adhere to the rules in order to survive. But it didn't matter; we would figure out a way. I looked at Isabelle and smiled; I would keep this plan a secret for now.

We streamed out and formed groups according to our respective duties. Slightly unsure of what we should do, we followed one another sheepishly until we reached our normal meeting places for duty. I said goodbye to Isabelle and went with Marc toward Alix's hut.

We followed the rest of the fire duty group through a darkened corridor to a large wooden door which led out into the monastery gardens. We gathered behind the door, remaining in the darkness, unsure if we should venture outside the building itself.

Suddenly, a loud shout thundered through the corridor from behind us, causing us to jump in fright in the already tense moment. In response, the door slowly opened, and bright light burst through. The silhouette of a soldier stood in the doorway before us, the outline of his rifle pointing menacingly towards us. He stepped aside to let us out into the snowy grounds.

We walked out along the familiar paths towards Alix's cabin and the wood stores. As we were walking along the snow-covered pathways, I stopped still, looking at the cabin ahead of us.

"What are you doing?" Marc asked, stopping and turning towards me. I pointed up to the cabin in response.

"No smoke," I said quietly. He looked up and stared. One of the few joys I had discovered here was walking into the woodcutter's cabin and being welcomed by the warmth of a roaring wood stove.

"Come on," he said and continued up the path ahead of me.

We reached the hut, but Alix was nowhere to be found. I looked toward the woods longingly. He must still be out there somewhere. Two soldiers stood, guarding the path leading into the field and the woods beyond. Evidently, they were preventing access to the wood as well as any form of escape. But if we could get past them, we would be free.

We organised ourselves into pairs. I went with Marc. Typically, a group of us would collect wood, but since that wasn't an option, we loaded up sacks with dried logs.

I looked at the soldiers who were blocking our path to freedom again. They looked fierce and insurmountable. Defeat washed up against the shores of my mind. I had no idea how we would get past them. I looked beyond them toward the woods. My thoughts rested with Alix, and I said a short prayer for his safety.

CHAPTER 21

*L*ife continued for us with relative normalcy over the following few weeks, just as Isabelle had predicted with her young yet wise mind. Fire duty remained the same, but we were no longer allowed to venture into the woods. Instead, our focus shifted to keeping the fires burning brightly using our ample stores. Alix was presumed to be trapped in the wood, and I couldn't help but worry for him. However, if anyone could survive in the wilderness by himself, it was Alix. I hoped that he had managed to escape and find help, but so far, no aid had arrived. Even if help did come, I doubted whether they could take on an elite unit of the German army.

During my trips to gather supplies for fire duty, I noticed something frustrating and worrisome. On a number of occasions, a group of men crossed the field to enter the woods. Most of them were soldiers, but there were two individuals with them who didn't carry any weapons, and their attire differed from that of the soldiers. They carried instead strange-looking boxes with wires and cables poking out. I didn't want more activity near the portal, as it would compli-cate my escape plan.

Every morning, I would climb up and peer out of the window next to Isabelle's bed. From that vantage point, I could just about spot the two soldiers guarding the field, but my view was limited. They were always there. One morning, with much frustration, I mentally set aside the plan for now and turned to Isabelle.

"Come on then, let's try and spend some time with Tom," I said, feeling renewed optimism for the success of her grand plan. We had made several attempts so far, but since the soldiers had taken over, it had become more challenging to convince Eric to leave his brother. His protective instincts had grown even stronger.

"You better prepare Marc then," she replied, pointing to Marc, who was lying lazily on his bed.

Before I could take a step toward him, the door burst open, and two German soldiers stormed into the room. They headed straight for Marc's bed, roughly grabbing him and dragging him out into the hallway. They commanded his presence for questioning. Everyone remained motionless and speechless, watching one of their own being taken away, fear silencing any resistance.

* * *

OUT IN THE HALLWAY, Marc managed to wriggle free from the soldier's firm grip.

"Get off!" he complained. Laughing, the soldier let him go.

"I have to make it look realistic," the soldier protested. "Come on, Captain Stahl wants to talk to you." After a while, the soldier gave Marc a sharp shove on his back. "Anyway, I can drag you all the way to the captain's quarters if I wanted. Don't get smart with us; you're just a little street rat," the soldier said dismissively. He walked toward Stahl's new rooms, with Marc following behind in renewed silence.

The soldier rapped on the door with his fist and stood patiently. The captain promptly signalled them to let Marc in.

Inside, a crackling fire burned strongly, with a neat pile of logs stacked to the side. Captain Stahl sat at a small writing desk with his back to the door. On the desk, glasses and bottles of wine were arranged, along with a pot of ink and stacked paper. The room boasted two large windows providing a suitable vantage point for monitoring outside activities.

Stahl hunched over some papers, scribbling something down. He placed his pen down and stood, turning to face Marc, who was still hovering by the open door.

"Ah, my little spy. Do come in and please shut that door," he gestured to Marc. Then, he turned his chair around and immediately sat back down. With no other seat available to Marc, he stood awkwardly.

"Well, let me cut to the chase," Stahl continued, omitting any pleasantries. "You said that you saw one of the children here open up that magic door. I need to know who that child is, and you're going to take me to him." He looked directly into Marc's eyes, his expression as cold as ice. The only warmth in the room came from the fire burning behind him.

Marc hesitantly shifted, averting eye contact with the captain.

"His..." Marc paused, then continued with much reluctance. "His name is Pierre." He looked at Stahl again, maintaining eye contact.

"Good," Stahl said, pulling out a piece of chocolate from his pocket and throwing it to Marc, who scrambled to catch the flying confectionery. Marc immediately secured it, stowing it deep into his clothes. "Let's go to this, Pierre, right now." Stahl got up from his chair, grabbed his coat, and led Marc out of the room. The two soldiers followed, and the dark captain led them back to Marc's dormitory, where Pierre was conspiring to make a new friend.

After a short pause, the soldiers roughly shoved Marc back into the room, causing him to stumble onto the stony floor. He got up, brushed himself down, and approached Pierre and Isabelle, who stared back at him in silence. The soldier hovering by the door then entered and headed straight toward the trio. He moved Marc aside and grabbed Pierre roughly by the arm.

"You, get your coat. You are coming with us," the soldier demanded, pulling Pierre away from Isabelle. Pierre turned back, mouthing that he would be okay. Marc wrapped his arms around the little girl, consoling her, as her friend was led outside into an unknown danger.

In silence, I was led outside into the grounds. Without uttering a word, they directed me along familiar paths, heading towards Alix's cabin. We continued past it and approached the two soldiers guarding the snow-covered field leading to the woods. They moved aside as we approached and stared at me menacingly as we walked past them and into the field.

Why were they taking me to the woods? Perhaps they had found Alix or knew he was hiding somewhere within, and they were questioning those on fire duty for answers. Puzzled, I wondered if they had also taken Marc into the woods—but he hadn't been gone long enough for that to be the case, and besides, he hadn't taken any outdoor attire.

We made our way, skidding at times, across the icy field toward the woods. I looked back at the monastery. The two soldiers had resumed their post, and the rocky monastery stood there, oblivious to the goings-on of the occupants inside and its new owners. I longed to be back in that place with my friends close by.

As we approached the woods, I stopped in my tracks, staring at a newly formed mound of dirt with a thin covering of frost and snow next to the path. The soldier behind me shoved me forward.

"Come on," he barked, disinterested in my need to pause. Although confused and burdened with unanswered questions, I obeyed his command and followed them into the woods.

A sense of dread began to wash over me as we progressed through the small forest. I realised we were heading straight for the tree that held the hidden doorway to the Endless World, my true home. No one knew about portals, so I didn't understand how that couldn't have been the case. This must be an unfortunate coincidence, I thought, trying to quell the rising panic. My heart raced as we crested a ridge, and the tree struck by lightning came into view. Two men dressed in white overalls held what appeared to be various scientific equipment and were studying the tree.

Questions flooded my mind. What were they doing? How did they know about the portal? The captain dressed in black stopped and turned to me.

"What's the matter? Have you just seen a ghost?" he asked theatrically. I looked up at him in shock. How did he know? With no response from me, he continued his questioning. "Do you recognise this place?" He grabbed my shoulders, his gaze piercing through my defences. I stumbled over my words, trying to protect the secret knowledge of the portal and the Endless World.

"Y-y-yes, I-I have spent a lot of time in this wood collecting firewood as part of my duties at the orphanage," I replied, looking back at him, hoping my efforts to conceal the truth would succeed.

"Why were you so disturbed when you saw the tree? What is so special about it?" I was unsure how to respond, my eyes shifting to the two men now examining the tree's bark.

"Nothing," I finally said, my voice feeble.

"I don't believe you," Stahl responded aggressively. He stood and pulled me sharply by my jacket collar, causing me to stumble and fall onto the cold, damp ground. "We know about the magic doorway, and we know about you, Pierre. We know you can open this door," he declared accusingly. No, it can't be. How does he know my name? How does he know about the portals? It wasn't possible, yet this nightmare continued to unfold before my eyes. Standing there dumbfounded, he continued to press me. "Open the door. Right now!" He demanded, looking at me expectantly. I glanced at him, then at the tree, and finally at the soldiers surrounding the wood. I couldn't comply; it would cause untold destruction.

"I don't understand," I feebly replied, hoping they would accept my obvious feint.

"I don't believe you," he said, letting go of my collar and reaching towards his pistol. He stopped, flexing his hand, restraining himself. "You see these scientists? They will open this magic door eventually. And when they do, you'll no longer have any value. If you simply open the door, we'll keep you and your friends safe from any harm." His hand still hovered by his gun, as if he was undecided on whether to use it or not. "Your time is running out, Pierre," he threatened. "Go back and think about my questions. When you're ready, you know where to find me." He nodded to his soldiers, who immediately responded by grabbing my arms and forcibly pushed me back towards the monastery.

The captain began conversing with the scientists as I was led away. We passed the mysterious mound in the field, the soldiers guarding the entrance, and the missing Alix's log cabin. Finally, we arrived back at my dormitory, which now stood vacant.

Left alone, I crumpled onto my bed. I would no longer be able to see my dad. A sudden realisation washed over me—the security I didn't even know I had been holding onto had been stripped away. Emptiness and loneliness consumed me.

I went over to Isabelle's bed and climbed up to look out at the guarding soldiers. I would need to escalate the escape plans, but I needed help. I decided to share my plan with Isabelle and Marc. There was no choice left; it was time to act. If only I knew then what I know now, the gravity of the mistake I was about to make.

CHAPTER 22

*W*e awoke the next day with darkness still enveloping the monastery. Despite the hour, the sounds and stirrings of life echoed through the halls. As we readied ourselves for the uncertain day ahead, the first rays of light pierced through our dormitory windows. I climbed up next to Isabelle's bed and peered outside, my eyes captivated by the emerging dawn. The sky, clear and vast, bathed the icy landscape in hues of soft pink. It was beautiful, and the present troubles momentarily evaporated from my mind. My father told me how natural beauty, or the "Lord's creation" as he often called it, would draw the admirer to a place where somehow sorrow could not be found. He explained to me that it was because in the Endless World, there was no sorrow, a place covered in this beauty, and that it was a bit like seeing glimpses into that wondrous place.

But as my gaze roamed the scene, it collided with the elongated shadows cast by the soldiers guarding the field. Their presence shattered my reverie, and my plan for escape and the unsolved challenges that went with it rushed back to the forefront of my mind.

"Isabelle," I called out to my little friend, who was busy by my side.

"Yes," she replied without looking up.

"There's something I need to tell you." Intrigue lit up her eyes as she glanced up at me.

"OK, what is it?"

"I think I have a way out of this nightmarish situation that we find ourselves in," I spoke with a serious tone. She met my gaze, silently urging me to continue.

"Promise me you won't tell anyone, Isabelle. It's of utmost importance that no one finds out what I'm about to tell you."

"OK, sure, what is it?" She repeated, her curiosity piqued. But doubt crept into my mind as I prepared to reveal the truth. The idea that I belonged to another world and was a prince with the ability to open magical doorways all seemed ludicrous. I reminisced about the day my father first showed me the portal in that cave long ago and how long it took for me to accept that reality despite the tangible proof in front of me. This time, I had to get Isabelle to believe me without witnessing the opening of a portal for herself.

"You know how I would often disappear during fire duty? Well, I wasn't always actually collecting wood." Isabelle stared blankly, waiting for me to explain. "I was going to see my father."

"What?" Her voice held disbelief. "Your father has been here this whole time?" Her astonishment echoed through the room. "Why didn't you tell us? What is he doing here?"

"Sorry, Isabelle. It's not like that. He isn't physically here, but he visits me in the woods." I struggled to find the right words to describe his visits, but Isabelle helped me piece it together.

"He must be nearby to be able to visit. I don't quite understand, Pierre."

"In the woods, there's a secret door that my dad comes

through." Her expression told me I had lost her completely as if she contemplated whether or not I was playing an elaborate prank. "Let me start from the beginning, and you'll have to trust me, okay?" I said, striving to maintain a serious demeanour. Met with her continued puzzled look, I explained how my father had shown me how to open a portal, revealing the existence of the Endless World and my true identity as a prince. I recounted how my father chose to place me at this monastery because of its proximity to the portal and that when he visited, he would leave acorns from the Endless World as a sign of his presence. I emphasised the importance of secrecy in order to protect our way of life.

"I'm sorry I didn't say anything before, but hopefully, you understand why."

"I don't know if I understand, Pierre, but I'll try," Isabelle replied, choosing to trust my incredible claims.

The bell began to toll, summoning us to breakfast. Before joining the rest of our dormitory in the great hall, I held onto Isabelle's arm. She turned toward me, and I revealed the remaining parts of my story.

"There's more. Yesterday, the Nazi captain took me to the exact location of the portal in the woods and demanded that I open it for him." Her face registered shock and alarm. "I haven't told a soul until now, Isabelle. I have no idea how he knows about it or about me." Panic tinged my words. "But the fact remains—he knows. We have to escape, and we can do it using the portal. But I can't do it alone, nor do I want to leave you or our friends behind. The problem is the constant surveillance guarding the entrance to the woods. We can't reach the portal without getting past them."

"We'll figure something out," Isabelle replied, surprisingly optimistic yet naive.

"They have scientists out there with some sort of equipment. I'm not sure if they'll be able to open the portal. Either way, we don't have much time." Fretting, I realised I lacked a concrete plan.

"Come on, let's go. We'll find a way," she replied, undeterred.

Marc suddenly appeared in the doorway.

"What are you two discussing?" he asked, his brows furrowed. Isabelle and I exchanged glances. We needed Marc's help, too.

"We're going to escape, Marc, and we want you to come with us. Are you in?" I asked, offering to explain everything as we made our way to the food hall. His expression remained flat and unmoved, but then, he grinned.

"Of course!" he replied, accepting my offer. We continued down the hallways toward the great hall, now recounting my story to Marc, elaborating on the portals and the urgency of our escape.

CHAPTER 23

*A*nother restless, sleepless night plagued Johan Baumann. It was the third in a row. Each time, he awoke with a vivid image etched into his mind, preventing him from finding rest—the serene, blue eyes of the monk he had buried. They stared at him peacefully, two clear pools of calm and tranquillity. No matter how hard he tried, he couldn't banish them from his mind whenever he closed his eyes.

Dealing with death was not new to First Lieutenant Baumann, but this time it affected him differently. Those eyes haunted him relentlessly, even in the waking moments of the day. He saw them every time he closed his eyes, even if briefly.

He lay still in his chamber, staring at the dark ceiling. The dying embers of the once roaring fire cast a gentle glow, allowing him to discern the vague outlines of shapes in the room. With a sigh, he climbed out of bed and sat there for a moment, lost in his thoughts.

Baumann went over to the fireplace and placed a couple of dry logs on top. He poked the wood and embers, stirring the flame to life once again. Adorning a gown, he approached the sole window and gazed out at the starry night sky. The majestic scene illuminated the snow-covered mountains in a cool blue and silver glow.

As he looked out, a sense of calmness washed over him. There was something about the nature of the night that reminded him of a more peaceful time in his childhood. Though he couldn't quite grasp the source of that feeling, it brought him a measure of rest. He moved back to his bed, sitting up with his back against the headboard, allowing himself to continue gazing at the stars through the small gap in the window.

Suddenly, a sharp, loud knock on the heavy chamber door jolted Baumann from his apparent slumber. Bewildered, he questioned how long he had slept. Although it was still dark outside, it was clearly becoming lighter. He couldn't afford to be seen by his men or anyone else in his nightgown.

"What is it?" he barked through the door, feigning annoyance to convey a clear message. He swiftly put on his uniform, preparing to face whoever was outside.

"Sir, Captain Stahl has requested your presence in his rooms for breakfast," a muffled voice replied from behind the door.

"Thank you. I'll be there shortly," Baumann dismissed the soldier. He finished getting ready and hastened to join his superior, knowing he should not keep him waiting. He reached for the door handle and began opening it. And there they were again—those beautiful blue eyes—this time, appearing like a hallucination on the back of the door. Startled, Baumann gasped in fear and jumped back, steadying himself against the cold stone wall. After a few moments of heavy breathing, he looked back at the door, but the face had vanished, leaving behind the plain wooden door. Shaking his head as if trying to dispel the madness, he exited and headed towards Stahl's room and to breakfast.

"Take a seat," Captain Stahl commanded, his mouth full of toast and poached eggs, as he pointed to a plate of food in front of Baumann. The first lieutenant complied, staring at the breakfast before him. His appetite wasn't quite there, but he forced himself to eat. Stahl looked at him intently and remarked, "Do you have everything under control? It looks like you've seen a ghoul."

Baumann looked up, meeting Stahl's stare. "Of course, sir," he replied quickly and dismissively. "What do you need today?" He resumed eating, fighting off the morning nausea.

"I want you to follow that Pierre boy," Stahl said, taking another bite before continuing. "Keep a sharp eye on him. The scientists believe we're mere hours away from opening the magic door, but there hasn't been much success yet. We need that boy; he's the missing key. Convince him to open that door," Stahl instructed, looking directly at Baumann.

"Yes, sir. I'll go to him right away," the first lieutenant affirmed. He stood up, saluted his captain, and robotically repeated the salute towards a portrait of their Führer hanging on the chamber wall.

Baumann left the captain's room intending to locate the boy and pursue his new objective. However, instead of heading to the food hall, he made his way directly to the nearest bathroom. Once inside, he entered a vacant stall and expelled his morning breakfast. Sitting on the stall floor, he felt dizzy and breathed heavily.

As he sat there, he questioned his path and the decisions that had led him there. He was at a crossroads where he could either continue on the same path or choose a different one. Sometimes, the choice might be obvious and simple, and the reward is substantial, but other times, like now for the first lieutenant, starting a new path would require great bravery and the reward unknown. Yet, choosing the right path would have an eternal impact, shaping the world for the better.

Baumann stood at this metaphorical fork in the road, staring at the new path in his mind's eye. He closed his eyes, and the blue eyes again stared back at him. "Argh!" he shouted in frustration. Rising to his feet, he slapped his hand against the stone wall, struggling with conflicting thoughts. A good soldier obeys commands and doesn't question them. This is war—a dark game that demands dark deeds. He walked over to the sink, cupped icy water in his hands, and splashed it over his face.

"I'm a good soldier," he told himself, repeating the phrase. He straightened his uniform, resolute in his decision. He barked a "Heil Hitler" to the empty bathroom, repeating it three times, each time louder than the last. Finally, he moved to the door, gripping the iron handle. He twisted it, paused for a moment, and closed his eyes; this time, blackness greeted him. Leaving the bathroom, he made his way to the food hall, determined to pursue his objective, unaware of the missed opportunity to embark on a new path—one that could have led away from a destiny of destruction and misery.

CHAPTER 24

*I*sabelle, Marc, and I ate our breakfast in silence, our minds consumed by the revelation of portals and the secret hidden world they concealed. Many questions bubbled to the surface, but Isabelle and Marc knew we would have to wait until we were alone to discuss them.

Leaning over to whisper, Isabelle shared an idea. "We need a way to discuss this without drawing attention. I propose we talk about a 'plan', and if anyone asks, we can simply say, 'Oh, it's a plan to get to spend time with Thomas, Eric's brother.' I guarantee everyone will understand that." We nodded in agreement, aware of the need for caution. However, I wasn't sure how long we could afford to be discreet. Perhaps discretion was a luxury unavailable to us now. I exchanged a concerned glance with Marc as we looked over at Eric and his brother across the hall.

"We will need to get Eric in on it," Marc said assertively. A pang of dread stabbed me from within. This was my most precious secret, and now not only did people know about it, but they also wanted to involve others, including someone I didn't trust. I looked at Marc, astonished. "Eric!?" I whispered angrily, trying to keep our conversation quiet. "He's the last person we should tell. He'll tell everyone! He won't take it seriously and will think it's some kind of setup."

"Hear me out," Marc responded calmly. "We are dealing with well-trained soldiers. We're just children. We need someone with experience who might have been in a fight before. Look, I don't want to interact with Eric if I can avoid it, but let's be real; he would be of great help if we managed to get him on our side." I looked at Isabelle, seeking her reaction. We both stared in silence, agreeing with Marc's persuasive reasoning.

Before any further consultation, Isabelle hopped off the bench and headed straight toward Eric and his younger brother. Speechless, we watched as she navigated between the long tables and started a conversation with them. Isabelle pointed to Marc and me, catching the brothers' attention. Eric gesticulated aggressively while Tom shifted uncomfortably in his seat. Eric seemed to scoff and ridicule Isabelle, dismissing whatever she was saying. Marc began to stand, his fists clenching. I grabbed his arm, nodding subtly toward the soldiers scattered around the room, reminding him not to cause a scene. He looked around, contemplating his next move.

Just then, the door burst open, and First Lieutenant Baumann stormed in, evidently angry. The entire room fell silent as everyone turned to watch the scene unfold. The commanding soldier scanned the room, searching for someone. His gaze abruptly locked with mine, and he headed straight toward me. Panic surged through me as I looked around nervously, wondering why he was coming for me. Had they figured out how to open the portal? I looked at Marc, panic-stricken.

The soldier grabbed the scruff of my neck and awkwardly dragged me away from the bench. I tried to stand and walk, but his grip was too tight, and I skidded along the smooth stone slabs. Desperately searching for someone to help, I could only find fearful and concerned faces until my eyes spotted Isabelle, tears streaming down her cheeks. Even Eric looked worried as I was forcefully dragged out of the great hall. Without a word, I was taken back along the narrow hallways to my dormitory. At the door, the Baumann threw me in. I skidded along the hard floor, struggling to stand and prevent an injury. Despite my best efforts, I hit my shoulder hard on the stone floor. Tears welled up as I clutched it in agony.

"Get your coat and any outdoor wear. We're going to your magic door," the German demanded, uncaring of any pain I might have been in. I stood, rubbing my shoulder in an attempt to ease the sharp, stabbing pains. Luckily, I soon realised there wasn't any serious damage, and I could carefully rotate my arm. Trembling, I obediently gathered my belongings, grimacing in pain with each movement.

We made our way to the woods and the special hollow tree, blackened by a lightning strike years before. As we arrived, the scientists were busy conducting their analysis, probing the tree for insights. Wires connected the tree trunk to various points on the ground and to a shoebox-sized machine that emitted whirring and clicking sounds. It produced a series of beeps, and a needle on a dial began moving erratically. The two scientists stood in anticipation, watching a specific area in the air in the exact spot where I knew the door to be located. The air began to shimmer, reminiscent of how the air looks above a flickering flame. As the distortion grew more substantial, so did my fear that they were about to open the doorway to the Endless World. Suddenly, the shimmering stopped, and the device with the dial and wires emitted a long beep lasting a few seconds. The two men cursed in frustration, attending to the machine.

One of them made adjustments, while the other repositioned some of the pegged wires on the ground.

"Young man," Baumann said menacingly. "It's time you tell us the secret to unlocking the door." I glanced at the scientists, then back at the soldier. His face seemed to have its own kind of distortion, a corruption I hadn't noticed before.

"No," I said defiantly, looking at the spot where the scientists stood and the air had moved. I lifted my gaze to the soldier, his face now contorted with rage.

He slapped me across the face, and I fell to the ground, pain flashing through my jaw as I tasted blood in my mouth. He yanked me back to my feet. "Tell me the secret to this door," he demanded once again. Despite trembling in fear and pain, I remained resolute.

"No," I repeated, wincing in anticipation of the next blow. But it didn't come. Slowly, I lowered my arms and cautiously opened my eyes to peer at the monster in front of me. His hand had lowered, but his face was still red with rage.

"Fine!" he screamed at me. "There are other ways to make someone talk." He stared at me menacingly. "Let's take a trip back to the orphanage and find someone who might help you reveal your secrets to me."

Relief washed over me, knowing that I wouldn't be struck again, but it was quickly followed by shame and guilt as I realised that someone else would now be in danger due to my silence. Dread settled in as I thought of little Isabelle. I had become something of a big brother to her, and that meant doing everything in my power to prevent harm from coming her way.

CHAPTER 25

"*I* told you!" Isabelle exclaimed as Eric stared at Pierre, who was being dragged out of the food hall by the scruff of his neck.

"Well, you are right. They are interested in Pierre," Eric said quietly, his voice now filled with concern. "But, I don't believe in this mythical nonsense of these portals. You're telling me that you've actually seen Pierre open up a secret portal that is a doorway to another world?" he asked incredulously. Isabelle looked at Eric, dumbfounded. "I mean, you have actually seen it, right?"

"No, not exactly," Isabelle replied hesitantly in a voice like a mouse. Eric started laughing.

"So, you want me to help you despite your plan being based on a fairytale that Pierre clearly made up? And you believed him without any proof?" he asked mockingly.

"It's true! Pierre has no reason to lie," Isabelle rebuffed, but this only caused Eric to laugh even more. Isabelle looked toward Thomas, hoping for some support. Thomas looked at his older brother, started to feign a chuckle, and then added quietly.

"I...I believe her," Isabelle smiled in response.

Before Eric could challenge them further, Marc suddenly appeared.

"It's true. Isabelle is telling the truth," Marc said, joining the conversation. Isabelle's small smile grew wider.

"Oh, not you as well?" Eric asked, mystified. "I don't know what game you're playing, but I'm not interested." Gesturing toward the door where Baumann had taken Pierre. "He could have just wanted Pierre to light a couple of fires for all we know."

"You know that's not true," Marc retorted hotly. "The German dragged him out with force. A bit excessive for a simple request to light a fire, don't you think?"

Eric scoffed in response.

"Look," Marc continued, "Pierre is in danger. We are in danger. We have to escape, and we need your help. If you're in, then after breakfast, let's meet back at our dorm to plan this thing." Marc extended the offer to Eric.

Eric paused for a short while before responding. "You're right that you will need me for this to work. I don't believe the silly game you're playing regarding the fairy doors, but I do want to get out of here— and I suppose I don't have anything better to do." Marc nodded in acknowledgement of Eric's terms. "My brother is coming too," Eric quickly added.

"Of course," replied Marc. He then turned to the others sat at Eric's table. "Hey, I know you've all been listening in. Do you want to come too?" The rest of them looked at each other with sheepish grins and nodded in agreement.

As word spread, a few more were recruited for this no longer-so-secret mission, but time was of the essence, and they needed all the help they could get.

Once gathered back at the dormitory, the room was now full of children, clambering about and finding available space to sit.

Isabelle stood on her bed to address the room. Still shorter than some of those standing next to the bed, she had to speak up in order to be heard.

"Listen up!" she called out. "If we are going to succeed, we will all need to stick and work together if we are going to escape from this place."

One of the girls she recognised, but didn't know her name, asked a question.

"The Germans are guarding this place tightly. How do you think we can do this? Even if we somehow get out of here, they'll hunt us down. And even if they can't find us, the cold will be sure to get us." Isabelle nodded, fully understanding the girl's concerns as she had repeatedly raised the same questions.

"You are quite correct to have these doubts. To answer your first question, we're not sure yet how to evade the constant watch of the soldiers, but this is what we are exploring now. In terms of where to go and what will happen after, Pierre has organised help for us in the woods. We'll be safe if we can just get to the wood on the other side of the great field." The room filled with murmuring as it received Isabelle's words.

"What is 'the help'?" someone called out.

"Help is out there. You'll have to trust us," Isabelle responded, hoping they would indeed trust. Eric himself stood up next to Isabelle on her bed to also address the audience.

"I don't know what the help is, if any. But what choice do we have?" he asked, wanting to progress the chat and discuss the plan. He climbed down, giving Isabelle a wink. Her heart filled with warmth at the surprising contribution from Eric.

"OK, any ideas?" Isabelle opened up the floor. A young lad, not much older than Isabelle, stepped forward.

"We could fight them. There are more of us than there are

of them; we could overpower them," he confidently suggested.

"They'll shoot us all," Marc stepped forward, batting down the suggestion. "They all have guns." The young boy sat back down, disappointed.

"What about asking the monks to help?" another boy piped up.

"I thought about this too," replied Isabelle, "but they might inform the soldiers."

"Alix would help," the boy continued. "He's different from the other monks."

"He is indeed," Marc interjected. "However, no one has seen him since the Germans arrived."

A long pause followed as all available options seemed futile, and as any and all suggestions were being refused, the children became reluctant to step forward.

"A diversion," a small voice said.

"What was that? You need to speak up," Isabelle replied, unable to hear what had been said.

"A diversion," Thomas repeated, stepping forward and speaking boldly. Isabelle nodded and smiled, encouraging him to continue. He climbed up onto the bed, standing next to Isabelle, and spoke out. "We won't be able to fight the soldiers. One or two of us could maybe sneak past the guards and escape, but to get all of us out, …then we would need a diversion." With no rebuttal from his audience, Thomas continued with renewed confidence. "I'm ashamed to admit this, but my father would often steal from the liquor shop in our town, and he would use my brother and me to create a distraction that enabled him to conceal a bottle or two. One time, we knocked over a display of matchboxes, and the shopkeeper cursed us while we pleaded it was an accident. As he re-stacked the display, my father stole four bottles!"

The young minds in the group were shocked by the

cruelty of the father to use his two sons in such a way, but Thomas didn't see it as such. Although he knew it was wrong, it was considered normal behaviour to him, and he believed that the other children must have had similar experiences. "Anyway, I propose we could do the same." He then climbed down, leaving Isabelle on her own again.

"I think that's the best option we have. Any ideas on how we can cause such a distraction?" she said, again opening up the floor for suggestions.

"I do," Marc said quickly, stepping forward. "I've noticed the soldiers each carry a grenade, sometimes two strapped to their sides. They are easily detachable and have long wooden handles. I'm confident I could steal one without being caught."

"Hang on, hang on," Eric interrupted, bemused. "Why won't you get caught? This simple detail puts everything at risk. It's not exactly easy to pilfer something from someone without them noticing," Eric asked, insinuating his previous failed attempts at similar tasks.

"You make a good point. We all have our secrets, Eric. You and your brother have yours. I have mine. Let's just say this won't be a problem for me," Marc replied, causing Isabelle to stare at her friend, who was becoming a stranger. "Anyway, we all have our duties. I'm on fire duty, and Isabelle here is on dorm duty. We all have a reason to be moving around on some errand. I could be on my way to light fires, and Isabelle could be collecting bedding. Those on kitchen duty could be picking winter vegetables in the allotments, and so on." Isabelle's mind came alive with ideas as Marc spoke.

"Yes! We could all meet at Alix's cabin. It has been empty since the soldiers arrived. No one should be there, so it should be safe," she chimed in enthusiastically.

"The wood stores are next to the cabin, so those on fire

duty are often right next to it anyway. Works for me," Eric added, content with his part of the assignment.

"The allotments are nearby too, so it works for those on kitchen duty," a tall, skinny boy Isabelle hadn't seen before chimed in. She nodded in delight as their plan was beginning to come together.

"Those on dorm duty often use the garden paths to get to the other side of the monastery as it's quicker. Going via Alix's cabin wouldn't be out of the ordinary," confirmed another. As the noise in the room rose with excited whispers, Marc stood up to solidify the plan.

"At an arranged time, everyone must find a reason to get to Alix's cabin. I will steal a grenade from a soldier, and when we're ready—set it off. We won't have long, though, once I've taken it, as the soldier would likely notice it's missing. When you hear the explosion, stay put. You need to wait for the two guards on watch over the field to leave their post. Then, when the coast is clear, run. Run like you've never run before, and then keep running like your life depends on it because it might. If you can reach the wood, then we're safe."

"Where will you be?" Eric asked. Marc paused for a moment.

"It'll be riskier for me. When I set off the grenade, I will only have a few seconds before it goes boom. I'm going to throw it and hide. I'll be near the cabin and will find a way to join you," Marc responded.

Isabelle's face darkened with concern. The once-perfect plan was now fraught with danger and would not be as easy to execute as she had previously thought. She tugged on Marc's sleeve.

"You will be safe, right?" she asked, her voice filled with worry.

"Of course! I'll figure it out," Marc said, quickly dismissing her concern.

Suddenly, one of the girls standing near the dormitory door shouted to the room in a loud whisper, "Soldiers! Quick!" She ducked out and disappeared down the hall right away. Others followed suit, while others remained busy, pretending to belong inside the dormitory. Moments later, the sound of heavy boots filled the hallway outside, echoes bouncing off the stone walls, growing louder and louder.

First Lieutenant Baumann appeared at the door with a shaken but intact Pierre firmly in his grip.

* * *

THE LIEUTENANT SHOVED me against the wall and held me there for a few moments. A protruding rock painfully dug into my back. Without saying anything, he let go and turned around, heading straight for the wide-eyed Isabelle sitting on her bed. Marc stood between them.

"Move," the German barked.

Marc feigned acknowledgement and reluctantly moved. Baumann continued toward Isabelle, pushing Marc aside effortlessly. Marc got to his feet and ran over to me.

"Get to Alix's cabin," he whispered into my ear. I looked at him, confused. He grinned back and looked down to show me the wooden handle of a grenade concealed under his jumper. I stared at him in shock as he ran out of the dormitory. My eyes quickly shot back to Baumann, who towered over a frightened Isabelle. He grabbed her viciously and carried her back to me like she was a sack of oats. I stared at his belt as I noticed only one grenade when, moments before, there had been two. The escape plan was in motion!

"Right, boy. Perhaps you'll show me now," Baumann said sarcastically, dangling Isabelle in front of me as a bargaining chip.

Making eye contact with the terrified little girl, I cried

out to make him stop. Baumann laughed gleefully at the ease of making me fold.

"It appears to me that I may have what I need to make sure you open that damned door," he continued, his voice reflecting his derangement. I looked at the man standing before me, completely unhinged.

He dragged us both into the hallway and then out into the cold air outside. Baumann was almost running as he pulled us along. Thinking desperately, I remembered my encounter with Marc moments before and his instruction to get to Alix's cabin. As we turned the corner, the cabin came into view.

"Wait!" I called out. Ignoring my protest, Baumann continued, determined as ever. "Wait! I need my special tool," I shouted in desperation. Baumann abruptly stopped and turned to me in frustration.

"Your what?" he demanded.

"To open the door, I keep a special tool hidden in that monk's cabin. It's a key of sorts," I quickly declared. The soldier responded enraged.

"You better not be lying, boy!" he screamed threateningly. I looked at Isabelle and back at the demented man, then quickly shook my head.

We reached the steps to the cabin immediately, and he threw me up them, causing me to trip and stumble and bash my shins against a protruding stone slab. Sharp pains shot through my legs, but I ignored them, desperate to avoid further wrath from the man.

"Hurry!" he shouted at me while gripping poor Isabelle in an iron-like vice. I ran inside, having no idea what to present if Marc's plan failed. Before I could think further, I was greeted by a number of children who had somehow managed to make their way to the wooden hut. Looking around in a panic, I restrained my voice from rising too much, asking:

"What's the plan?"

"Marc has a grenade. He's going to use it to create a diversion. Then, when it's clear, we head to the wood. You have help for us there," Eric answered plainly.

I looked at their faces. They had placed their hope in this plan and in me. I peered through the small window, the large frame of Baumann standing outside, clutching Isabelle tightly. I looked at the faces of the children in the cabin again.

"I can help. In the woods, I can get all of you to safety," I said, confirming their hope. We now needed Marc to pull through.

"Knock, knock!" Baumann suddenly called from the other side of the door and pushed it open menacingly.

"Well, well, well. What do we have here?" He threw Isabelle to the floor and slammed the door shut. He looked around at the cowering faces, his eyes wide with madness. Another sound came from the other side of the door.

"Ah, someone else has come to join us!" Baumann exclaimed, his voice filled with mania. He skipped to the door excitedly and opened it.

In the doorway stood the captain, dressed in all black, silhouetted by the bright light behind him. Beside him stood Marc, clutching onto the lieutenant's grenade.

CHAPTER 26

*T*here are few moments in life where the rug is cleanly taken from under your feet, leaving you dumbfounded and searching for solid ground. Betrayal is a particularly foul weapon, requiring a level of intimacy and trust that leaves susceptible minds vulnerable to attack. Unfortunately, those with trusting minds fail to realise the assault made upon them, continuing to trust their betrayer. And so it was, the collective response of us all seated there, staring at our young friend, Marc, holding the grenade. The rug had been swept away, and we stood, unable to recognise the fact that Marc had betrayed us.

We urged Marc to launch the grenade. The German captain laughed hysterically at our expense and patted Marc's head gently.

"Good boy," he said as if to an obedient pet dog.

With a hint of regret, Marc offered the grenade back to Baumann, who gleefully snatched it from him and reattached it to his side.

Confusion clouded my mind as I stared at Marc. We had

all been tricked, but I couldn't fully comprehend it. A slight tug on my sleeve caught my attention. I looked down to find Eric sitting there, his expression filled with sadness.

"He got us all, even me," he said, his voice filled with regret. "I can usually spot liars a mile off, but apparently not this time."

Not knowing what to say, I turned my gaze back to Marc, finally realising that the rug had been well and truly pulled out from under us.

"Listen up, you fools!" Captain Stahl suddenly shouted. We all stared at the man in unison, dumbfounded, fear once again forcing us into obedience.

He placed his arm around Marc, a sickening display of fondness. "Young Marcus, here, is an example for you all. He is strong, and you are weak. He is wise, and you are stupid. He has informed us of all your schemes, plans, and more right from the beginning. And now, he has cleverly trapped you all here with no escape! Brilliant!" He looked about, clearly proud of himself. "If you were as wise as I am, perhaps you would have noticed this obvious ploy. Alas, once a fool, always a fool. You are all weak, and I have no time for weak fools."

Two soldiers emerged from behind the captain and began cuffing each of us, one by one. Two trucks suddenly appeared outside, their engines rumbling loudly and shaking the ground beneath us. Bewilderment washed over us all. Where had these trucks come from? We were roughly brought to our feet, ready to be put into the awaiting vehicles.

* * *

ERIC POSITIONED himself in front of his younger brother, instinctively acting as a shield between him and the

141

approaching soldiers. At that moment, a realisation flashed into Eric's troubled mind. He suddenly understood the truth behind all that I had spoken of—the importance of sticking together, helping those in need, and shaping our world despite the tough circumstances we might find ourselves in.

A vision sprang forth in his mind's eye. He saw his father as a young boy and witnessed his grandfather, his father's father, angrily shouting and pushing his dad around, just as Eric himself had experienced countless times growing up with his own father. The cycle was being repeated, and Eric could see the beginnings of it in himself in the way he treated Thomas. He knew then that the cycle had to be broken.

He glanced at his brother behind him and leaned over to kiss him on the forehead, silently apologising. Then, he turned to me.

"You were right," he said.

"Sorry, what do you mean?" I asked, confused.

"You were right," he repeated. "About everything."

Suddenly, he sprang into action, moving like a coiled snake attacking its prey. He seized a knife from the thigh of one of the approaching soldiers, its blade glistening in the light. Without hesitation, he thrust the knife back into the soldier's leg. The soldier shrieked and fell backwards. Eric grabbed me and shouted, "GO!"

In the midst of chaos and confusion, I leapt into action, running like a hare toward the exit. I hesitated as I reached the door, glancing back into the cabin. Captain Stahl held Eric down while the wounded soldier cursed loudly. The children were scrambling about, and I searched for Isabelle, unable to leave without her.

"Run, Pierre!" Eric shrieked, wild with desperation. Stahl looked up at me and pulled out his pistol. Without thinking, I turned and sprinted as fast as my legs could carry me out of the cabin and toward the snowy field. My feet skidded and slid as I desperately navigated my way across the courtyard paths.

BANG!

The sound of a gunshot echoed through the air. I felt a surge of adrenaline as I ran, my heart pounding in my chest. A moment later, Thomas's piercing screams reached my ears. I wanted to return to help my friends, but it was hopeless. Eric had given me a chance to escape, and I couldn't let it be in vain.

* * *

ANIMALISTIC INSTINCT TOOK over as I fled the brutal scene. My mind focused solely on reaching the portal as quickly as my legs could carry me. I raced across the pathways and through the gardens of the monastery, startling a group of unknowing soldiers as I dashed past them. Before they could react, Stahl burst through the cabin door, his Luger pistol in hand. Spittle formed at the corners of his mouth as anger surged through his veins. He turned to his men and screamed at them to stop me.

"Stop that boy! Shoot him!"

But, like a hare eluding capture from a predatory fox, I slipped past them, under a post and rail fence, and into the snowy field. Each step was now slow and heavy as my boots sank into the snow. It was reminiscent of a nightmare where, when being chased by a demon, you can't run. I stumbled, just as in the dream, and as I gathered myself, I looked back to see if my friends had made it. The settled snow muffled all sounds as I scanned the scene.

BANG!

The snow in front of me exploded, showering me with

white icy powder. My focus shifted to the smoking pistol in Stahl's hand. Swearing, he started running toward me once again. I turned and ran as fast as I could, heading into the woods through the gap in the stone wall. Two more shots rang out, peppering the tree next to me as I sprinted past it, tears now streaming down my face. My life could disappear in an instant.

The portal was just ahead. I could hear Stahl behind me, his footsteps crunching through the snow, growing closer. Panic gripped me as I threw my hands out; the air a few feet in front of me started to shimmer. A small circle of sunlight appeared, floating in the air. The crunching snow behind me stopped. Emmerich Stahl stood still, raising his pistol, his aim centred on my back. I dove through the opening as Stahl squeezed the trigger. The gun snapped back, firing the bullet.

I hit the ground hard, grazing my body against the floor. As I lay there, breathing heavily, I gently touched my side, my fingers coming away stained with blood. Confusion washed over me as I looked down. I felt no accompanying pain; the crimson red was not my blood. Whose was it? Could it be the man chasing me? I didn't think he had gotten that close. I glanced back at where the portal should have been, only to find the peaceful, breezy forest sprawling before me. There was no sign of danger.

My thoughts turned back to the world I had just left, to my friends. I had left Isabelle behind, and I had no choice. Instinct had taken over, guiding me to escape. I had no idea if any of them had made it, and even if they had, what would they do now? Adults, let alone children, didn't survive in freezing mountains without food, water, or shelter. I had to go back and help rescue them.

I held my hands out in the air, concentrating. Nothing happened. I had never tried to open a portal from the Endless World before. Perhaps it couldn't be done immediately or required a level of skill I had yet to attain. Frustrated, I tried again—still, nothing. Knowing I couldn't waste any more time, I turned around and started to run. I wasn't supposed to be here, but I had to find help, and I had to do it now. My father's voice echoed in my mind, his words warning me against returning to my home kingdom before my time on Earth was up. But I had no choice. My friends were in grave danger, and there had to be help here. Tears streamed down my face as a sense of helplessness washed over me, propelling me through the forest.

As I ran, I noticed splashes of red against the green leaves. Whose blood was it? I looked down at my shirt and kept running, dodging low branches and hopping over roots as I followed an ancient, worn trail. The blood spots continued to mark the path. Suddenly, I came to a halt in front of a tree blocking my way. I stared up at the trunk, a crimson handprint painting the bark. The blood belonged to a person, and in that moment, I knew whose.

"Papa."

Kneeling down, my knees sinking into a small red puddle, everything started to make sense. My father's absence during our planned meet-ups and Marc's betrayal—they all fell into place. I trusted Marc and believed he had my best interests at heart. He knew I had come to see my father. How could he do this? My carelessness allowed the German army to be stationed at the monastery, miles away from the war. They all knew, and it was all my fault. I hadn't been careful enough.

* * *

STAHL'S ARM EXTENDED, gun in hand, smoke swirling from the barrel.

"It's true," he murmured to himself, his eyes wide with

realisation. "Portals exist." A grin crept across his face, a mark of his descending madness. "This is how we will win," he declared, his voice tinged with insanity.

CHAPTER 27

*A*s I followed the trail, the dread and panic that consumed me at first slowly began to loosen its grip. In its place, a sense of peace and calmness washed over me, accompanied by an inexplicable feeling that everything would be alright. How could I find such solace in the midst of such dire circumstances?

Carefully treading the ancient pathways of the forest, I savoured the warmth of the still air. I recalled my father's words about time working differently here and how it seemed to slow down. This land was known as the realm of plenty, where time was endless. Lost in thought, I slowed my pace, pondering the nature of such a phenomenon.

As I continued, the breathtaking beauty of the place soothed my troubled soul. Descending a slight incline, the distant roar of a mighty river reached my ears. A pair of deer gracefully leapt across the path ahead, unfazed by my presence. I couldn't help but smile at their simple innocence. Yet, this serene moment didn't last, as drops of my father's blood on the soft ground reminded me of him and of my friends back at the distant orphanage. It's hard to explain to someone who has never set foot in this world, but despite the gravity of the situation, a sense of reassurance embraced me—a clarity of mind that acknowledged the situation while remaining steadfast in the belief that all would be well.

Reaching the edge of the forest, I surveyed the vast lands beyond. Rolling green hills stretched into the distance, their vibrant colours painting a picturesque landscape. Snow-capped mountains towered in the farthest reaches while the river I had heard earlier rushed to my right, meandering through the plains. Along its banks, roads crisscrossed, adorned with numerous bridges and dwellings; I wondered who inhabited those houses.

Stepping out into the meadow, I continued to follow the ancient trail. Towering, colourful wildflowers surrounded me while insects and bees danced in the air, creating a gentle symphony. Memories of warm summers spent fishing with my father flooded my mind. It was as if this place breathed life into my cherished recollections. As if those experiences were mere previews of this beautiful world.

Lost in my thoughts, I spotted a large stone structure in the distance. I halted in my tracks and surveyed the sprawling castle shrouded amidst the trees. Towering structures and intriguing dome shapes dotted the massive building in every direction.

The sound of distant thuds echoed like a quickened heartbeat, drawing my attention away from the giant building to an emerging rider on horseback up ahead. The rider was dressed regally in full armour, a large sword strapped to his back. The sun's rays gleamed upon the glistening armour, something akin to shimmering diamonds. The horse itself was dressed in beautiful and ornate attire, making it an exquisite sight to behold. They approached me directly, and rather than fear, I felt a deep sense of peace, a sense of belonging to this place, an unspoken assurance that this encounter would be as with a friend.

As he reached me, the knight dismounted, and both horse and rider kneeled before me, their postures filled with reverence.

"Your majesty," the knight greeted, his head bowed low, almost touching the ground.

I stood, uncertain of how to respond, as they remained in their humble positions.

"Um, yes?" I replied, hoping my words would suffice. The knight and his horse rose, maintaining an air of respect.

"Your majesty, it has been so long, and you have grown so much. It is a great joy to see you!" the knight exclaimed.

"Pardon me, sir, but I don't believe we've ever met," I responded, somewhat confused.

"Ah, yes, of course. I apologise; I often forget myself. You might not know this, but this isn't your first time here. You were actually born in this realm. When the royal family welcomes their firstborn, their work on Earth begins," the knight explained casually yet with the utmost respect.

"I was born here?" I asked, my voice filled with astonishment.

"Ah, little prince, there is much to teach you. Your mother, Her Royal Highness, insisted I fetch you without delay. Please, allow me to help you onto my faithful steed, and we shall return to the castle."

"My mother? She's alive?" I inquired, hope and disbelief mingling in my words.

"Prince Pierre, yes, she is indeed alive. It must be quite perplexing for you. The elders and scholars are better equipped to explain, and you'll have ample time to ask as many questions as your bravery allows. But for now, let me take you to your mother," the knight assured me.

With gentle guidance, the knight helped me onto his

steed, and we galloped down the meadow trail, heading toward the grand castle in the distance. All the while, I bombarded the knight with questions about my mother—what she was like, how she looked. Honoured and privileged to respond, the knight delighted in recounting every detail. Tears of joy welled in my eyes, uncontainable even in this place—the genuine expression of a young boy about to be reunited with a mother he had only dreamed about his whole life.

CHAPTER 28

$\mathcal{W}$e continued along the old trail, passing the occasional traveller. Each one bowed down on the side of the track as we went past. It intrigued me, and if I wasn't about to see my mother, I would have wanted to stop and meet each of these people.

"Who are they?" I asked the knight.

"These are your subjects. The people here once lived on Earth. They were born there, and then they came here to live."

"My subjects? I'd like to talk to some of them one day."

"There will be plenty of time for that, Your Majesty," the knight retorted, chuckling to himself.

He was forthcoming in answering all of my questions except one. He wouldn't tell me his name. I found this odd, but he replied that it didn't matter and that it would have to remain a mystery for now.

As the magnificent castle came into view, structures lined each side of it as far as the eye could see. It was the largest building I had ever come across. The river to our right snaked around and crossed in front of us, where a sizeable cobbled bridge led up to the castle. Its wooden doors were opened wide, welcoming all who wanted to enter.

The knight steered the horse to cross the stony bridge. I saw other knights, unique in appearance, stationed along the way, dressed in beautiful garb with various types of armour and weaponry. I glanced at the knight escorting me and the sword strapped to his back.

"All of you knights have such interesting swords, axes, bows, and other weapons. My father said this place is peaceful. Why do you need them?" I pondered.

"Young prince, you should sit down with the elders. They would love to tell you about these things. Alas, that will have to wait as your duty remains on Earth. But your questions require a better explanation. As a short answer, the Endless World isn't impervious to attack. It just hasn't happened before."

The knight's response filled me with even more questions. I looked at the river below, meandering about and appearing to travel directly under the castle.

"Is the castle floating?" I queried.

"Not quite, young prince. The river is special. There's actually a bigger castle than this one where the river flows from, if you can believe it." My imagination reached its limit.

"How could there be a bigger castle than this one?"

"Well, it also doesn't technically exist in the Endless World but in another realm beyond. But again, this is a topic for the elders and scholars."

As I tried to comprehend the concept of yet another world, we crossed over the bridge to the other side. We passed through the enormous archway of the open doors. Great chains and mechanical devices could be seen between the door and the connecting walls. Through the doors was a large open square full of light and colour. People laughed and engaged in conversation. Bright purple, yellow, red, and orange sheets stretched high up, creating warm colours as the sun shone from behind them.

We started to make our way through the bustling crowd when the conversation was suddenly silenced, and all attention was drawn to us. The crowd dropped to their knees, and silence descended upon the square, aside from the sheets flapping in the wind.

"Why is everyone kneeling?" I whispered.

"Your Majesty, these are your subjects, and you are their beloved prince."

"But they don't know me," I protested.

"Young prince, they know who you are and what you represent."

I looked about at all the people dressed in bright, attractive garb, not as sophisticated as the knight's attire but beautiful in its own way.

"Please, stand!" I called out as loudly as I could muster.

One by one, the people stood, their smiles and expressions of joy directed towards me. It was overwhelming. When my father told me I was a member of the royal family, it felt abstract. Now, I was experiencing the reality of it. Not knowing what to do, I waved and smiled back.

"Your Majesty, the Hall of Brave Ones is just up ahead here. And your mother will be in the throne rooms just beyond."

We exited the courtyard and entered a tunnel of sorts. To the left, a significant drop revealed the flowing river below, with two large wooden waterwheels turning, splashing water loudly. The horse's hooves clopped loudly on the stony floor, but it had a soothing effect on my soul. Light reflected off the water, casting interesting patterns on the ceiling and gently illuminating the tunnel.

As we continued along the downward tunnel, the stone floor almost level with the flowing river, it opened up into a large domed hall. Light burst through the ceiling and high walls in dazzling colours, courtesy of stained glass windows depicting stories of brave knights and princesses. The river split into multiple streams, and small bridges and pathways sprawled out amongst various trees and plantings, blurring the line between a room and a garden.

Benches were dotted about, and gardeners tended to the foliage. As we went past, they politely made room for us, bowing down. I greeted each one.

The prospect of seeing my mother in a few short moments was immense. I was eager to hurry straight to the throne room, but the beauty and intrigue of this place captivated me like nothing before.

"Hello there," I greeted two people who had stood up from a bench. As we passed them, I couldn't stop staring, turning my head to do so. They looked strikingly familiar. "Stop!" I commanded the knight, who abruptly brought his horse to a halt. Awkwardly, I clambered down and walked back to the two who had remained bowing.

Gently, I placed my hand under one of their chins and slowly lifted their head.

"Alix!" I exclaimed, greeted by his brilliant blue eyes and a warm, familiar smile.

"Your Majesty," he softly replied. "I knew there was something special about you."

"What are you doing here?" I asked, suddenly confused. The knight walked up from behind and gently put his hand on my shoulder.

"Young prince, we are in the Hall of Brave Ones. This is a very special place, where those who have committed great acts of bravery are honoured." He looked to Alix with an expression of genuine admiration but also regret. "Alix here did something very brave and made the ultimate sacrifice. He resides here now."

I looked towards Alix, a tear rolling down both our cheeks.

"Thank you," I said to him, "it's a great honour to see you again."

"The honour is all mine," he replied, chuckling.

I turned to the person on his right, their head still bowed in reverence.

"Stand," I commanded firmly yet kindly. They slowly stood and just as slowly lifted their head. "Eric!" I said with great joy, hugging him and struggling to believe they were really here.

"You were right all along, Pierre," Eric started. The knight coughed and shifted uncomfortably. "I'm sorry, Your Majesty," he quickly corrected himself.

"Don't be silly," I countered, "call me Pierre. That's an order." I was thrilled to see them both. I looked back at Alix. "You must have gone through the portal, Alix, but Eric, how did you get here? And before me? I've literally just come straight here, even on horseback." Alix and Eric looked at each other, unsure of what to say. The knight placed his hand on my shoulder.

"Come, Your Majesty, let's go and see Her Royal Highness," the knight suggested. I stood there, unmoving, trying to piece the puzzle together. After a short while, I turned to the knight.

"What happened? How did they get here?" I demanded, needing an answer.

"Let's leave these two here to rest, and we can discuss it on the way to your mother."

The knight helped me back onto the horse, and we set off once again.

"Young prince," the knight began, "there is more than one way to enter the Endless World. Obviously, you know how the portals work. It's a secret that only you and your family know. The other way is through one's death on Earth." The knight continued, and suddenly, it dawned on me what must have happened. "They were killed," I whispered quietly, my words trailing off. My heart went out to my other friends and the monks at the orphanage, hoping they were all safe.

"The mechanics of it all elude me, and this is another topic for the elders. Those residing in the Hall of Brave Ones committed great acts of bravery during their time on Earth and are honoured here. The people in this Hall are generally younger, as they tend to meet their end before their time." Numb and tired, I allowed the knight to continue his explanations as we headed away from the Hall of Brave Ones and into the royal throne rooms.

Two knights wearing identical armour and clothing guarded the entrance. The knight escorting me nodded, and they both bowed low, allowing us to pass. The knight then stopped his horse, and we dismounted.

A warm golden glow was emanating from the throne room ahead.

"This way," the knight said, placing his hand on my shoulder and gesturing me onward. We walked on together, leaving his horse behind. Silence enveloped my soul, with both deep joy and anticipation taking root. Everything else disappeared from my thoughts as we entered the large throne room. The knight halted, gave a bow and exclaimed, "Your Royal Highness, I present His Royal Highness, Prince Pierre the Third."

I looked around eagerly, the room bathed in a warm golden glow. Confusion filled me as I turned to the knight, seeking clarification. He nodded, urging me to step forward into the room. As I did so, I saw the source of the glow—a large spherical orb situated in an ornate golden stand. It swirled in blue and yellow hues, and standing next to it, staring intently, was my mother.

CHAPTER 29

*O*nce or twice in a lifetime, there are moments when everything falls away, and nothing else matters except for one thing.

When my mother turned to face me, nothing else mattered. We locked eyes and ran toward each other. She crouched and picked me up, swinging me around. She held me close, kissing my head.

"Pierre! It's so good to see you!" I didn't want her to let go. She took a step back to look at me. Her smile beamed down at me so warmly. Apart from my father, I had never encountered such genuine love from someone before.

She was wearing a pretty, elegant gown with a gem-studded golden crown upon her head. Her regal presence and beauty were captivating. Her eyes sparkled; I could see a mixture of joy and sadness, and her love for me was palpable.

Then I noticed it. A mark, spoiling the otherwise perfect scene. There was blood on her arms and gown, even upon her face. I wasn't quite sure how I had missed it before.

"Mother, there's blood on you," I said fearfully. She looked down in confusion.

"Ah yes, my dear one. Come here. I need to show you something." She gestured toward the glowing orb on its golden stand.

She placed her hand on the smooth surface. I would say it was made of glass, but I'm not so sure it actually was. It was a material I had never encountered before. As she touched it, the clouds of colour began to swirl quickly.

"What is this?" I asked, intrigued.

"If the portals are doors between worlds, this would be a window."

I stared at the majestic, swirling colours.

"How does it work?" I asked curiously.

"It's the same gift as the portal magic, my little prince. The difference is that there is only one of these orbs. You can look through it, but you cannot pass through. It is believed there were once many more orbs like this one out there, but they have since been lost in time."

I continued to stare into the orb, not fully understanding what my mother was saying. Suddenly, a faint image started to emerge within the sphere. I rubbed my eyes as if to remove any imagination from them. The picture slowly became clearer—it was of a room with many beds and people walking about. It was a hospital ward. The people walking about were nuns and nurses, and the beds held injured soldiers.

"It's a ward for injured soldiers," I said, almost questioning.

"That's right, Pierre. If you look closely, the man in the bed right in the middle, that's your father." I suddenly looked intently at the man. The missed rendezvous with my father, the trail of blood I stumbled into when being chased by that Nazi Captain—what happened to my father came wildly into focus at that moment.

"They shot him!" I exclaimed, worried.

My mother put her arm around my shoulders. "I wish I could be with him," she said sadly. I started to feel terrible for what had happened. I was reckless, took too much risk, and told someone about the secret. This was all my fault.

"I-I-I'm so sorry," I muttered feebly. My mother remained silent as she kept her eyes fixed on my father.

Like a seed blowing in the wind and landing in moist, fertile soil, guilt and shame immediately began developing roots inside my fragile and vulnerable mind.

"You will have to go back to Earth now," my mother said solemnly, turning to me.

I didn't want to leave, but I knew I had to in order to make things right again. Before I left, I had some unanswered questions.

"Why can't we bring him here to get better?" I asked in desperation.

"Pierre, his wounds are likely mortal," came my mother's reply.

"Mortal?"

"I'm sorry, my little prince, but he's likely going to die from his injuries. And he has to do that on Earth." The feelings of shame increased significantly.

"But why?" I protested.

"I wish we had the time to explain. We are a special family born in this realm. As you know, we have a duty to live out a life on Earth until death, and then we come back here and live another life. We have our duty on Earth, and while it is possible to travel between worlds, we must always honour our duty. There are consequences for stepping into this place before one's time. Your father is now suffering alone because of this."

"Father had to enter this place to see me," I said, attempting to justify the outcome.

"Yes, he did. It was against my wish, but he insisted. He

had to keep you safe. You are not performing your duty by staying here before your time, and ultimately, Earth suffers."

It was all my fault. Father had risked it all coming to see me. I was stupid enough to tell my friends about the portals and was betrayed by that snake Marc! Alix and Eric were both killed because of my selfishness. Isabelle was still in danger, and my father was about to die a painful death. I collapsed to the floor, bursting into tears and sobbing.

My mother wrapped her arms around me, attempting to console me.

I had to go back. I had to make it right. I had to fix what I had broken.

"Okay, I'm going to go back," I stood and looked toward the knight, who had been patiently standing in the shadows at the entrance. "Knight! Take me back to the portal," I called out.

"No," my mother interrupted softly. "You can't go back to the orphanage. It's too dangerous now," she said, looking at me regretfully.

"I have to. That must be my duty to make things right. My friends are still there. This is all my fault; I have to go back."

"No," she repeated.

I looked at my mother incredulously.

"But my friends—"

"I'm sorry, but we can't lose you too. You have to go back to your father. We have made arrangements for you to stay with a family when it is safe to do so. You will be kept safe until the end of the war, and you can continue your duty." I didn't know what to say. I very much wanted to see my father. I very much wanted to stay here and not return to Earth. I very much wanted to return and help Isabelle and my friends at the orphanage. My mother was right; I had to do my duty.

I hugged her tightly. I didn't want to let go. She held on,

too, thinking the same. Slowly, she faced me and kissed me on my forehead.

"Be brave, my little prince. I'll see you again soon." I smiled, and we hugged again.

I ran down the steps back to the knight.

"Wait!" my mother called out. "You don't know where to go. Nameless Knight, take Pierre to the great waterfall; he will discover the portal there." Bowing low, the knight accepted his new orders.

We left the throne room and headed out of the castle, back through the Hall of Brave Ones, out through the court-yards, and across the bridge to the ancient trails and pathways.

The knight started travelling upon a new route away from the castle.

"Stop," I commanded the knight. With a click from his mouth, he halted his horse. "Take me back to the meadow where you found me. I'm going to go back to the woods."

The knight turned to me, his face expressing great conflict.

"Young prince," he began calmly, hoping to bring some sense to me. "We can't go back to the wood. It's too dangerous to go through the portal there. It is safer for you to be with your father."

"I appreciate your concern, but I have friends at the orphanage who need me. What duty can I perform if I can't even help those closest to me? I can't just leave them. You're going to take me back there," I said firmly and, after a short pause, added, "That's an order."

The knight closed his eyes regretfully, made a couple of clicking sounds, and urged his horse forward. The horse turned and started galloping in the direction of the meadow and towards the forest.

CHAPTER 30

*S*creams erupted in the log cabin as the gunshot rang out. The children scattered, desperately trying to escape the chaos unfolding around them. Baumann, blocking the doorway, stood menacingly in their path.

"Quiet!" he screamed at the top of his lungs. The terrified children froze, surrendering like trapped animals in the jaws of a predator.

Commanding the soldiers present, the lieutenant rounded up the children and led them back to the monastery, leaving behind the injured soldier tending to his knife wound and the lifeless body of Eric.

All plans for escape seemed futile now, with Eric dead, Pierre missing, and Marc having betrayed them. The soldiers had allowed the children and monks to keep the monastery operational, but now they were under constant supervision, with a soldier posted outside each occupied dormitory at night.

It was unnecessary, as the captives had nowhere to go. The threat of punishment loomed over them, keeping them confined within the monastery walls.

Loneliness washed over Isabelle as she curled up in her bed, surrounded by constant reminders of the brutality of her situation. In her despair, her eyes searched for Thomas, who had fallen into complete silence following his brother's death.

She found him, his still figure gently illuminated by the moonlight. She wondered if he blamed her. She tried to talk to him, but he responded with a sad stare.

Her thoughts drifted to Pierre; no one had seen or heard from him since he ran. She hoped he had made it back to his home world and was returning with help. It was their only glimmer of hope.

Days blended together in a monotonous routine. The children woke each morning and went to the food hall for breakfast, followed by their assigned duties, lunch, more duties, dinner, and then bedtime. The conversation was minimal as everyone kept to themselves.

The German soldiers remained mostly uninvolved, except for the guards. Occasionally, Isabelle would catch glimpses of them disappearing into the woods across the field. It lifted her spirits slightly, as it likely meant Pierre had escaped, and they were still experimenting out there.

Isabelle pretended to be on fire duty, giving her an excuse to be close to Thomas despite his silence.

One snowy morning, she followed Thomas out into the gardens. They made their way to the wood store around the side of Alix's cabin. Snowflakes fell gently around them as they filled their empty baskets with logs and kindling.

Suddenly, Thomas put his arm protectively across Isabelle's chest. She looked at him fearfully. He pressed a finger to his lips, urging her to be silent. She glanced around and heard the captain and his lieutenant conversing as they walked past, towards the gate and the snowy field just around the corner.

Isabelle and Thomas crept as close as they dared, eavesdropping on their conversation.

"Today is a breakthrough day, Baumann," the captain said gleefully.

"They've cracked it?!" his lieutenant exclaimed.

"Mostly. They've managed to open it like a window, but it fades away when they get close, so they have to reset the experiment. The next phase is passing objects through," Stahl replied, grinning hungrily. "Come, I'll show you. The war will be ours, and we'll be handsomely rewarded." Captain Stahl turned to lead the way across the field.

"And we'll get that boy," Baumann finished grimly.

Isabelle urgently turned to Thomas. "We have to go. We have to stop them," she pleaded. Thomas stared back, shaking his head slowly. "Didn't you hear? Pierre escaped! They might be moments away from going after him," she whispered.

"No," Thomas said quietly. Isabelle stopped, shocked by his break in silence. "We can't," he whispered. He nodded toward something behind Isabelle. She turned and saw a soldier lurking nearby, his gun visible from the side. She looked back at Thomas, her face filled with turmoil.

"You're right," she agreed, her voice heavy with disappointment. Pierre had promised to get help. She had to trust his plan. There simply wasn't an alternative.

* * *

"Show the lieutenant what you showed me," Stahl ordered the scientists excitedly.

They smiled and began preparing the scene for their experiment. One of the scientists handed Baumann a pine cone, placing it carefully in his open palm.

"When it opens, throw this through," the scientist

instructed before hurrying off to complete various preparations. Captain Stahl and Lieutenant Baumann watched, eagerly awaiting the results. Wires were placed around the charred tree, covered in small coloured pins which were connected to each wire.

One scientist adjusted dials on a large box sitting on a wooden table. The machine whirred to life, lights flickering on and off. Another scientist rushed to Stahl and Baumann.

"Stand back," he instructed.

Captain Stahl observed the scientist for a moment before taking a step back. The lack of discipline and the absence of "please" or "sir" grated against his military ideals. He made a mental note to ensure that once the scientists were no longer needed, they would be sent away and disappear for good.

The ground beneath them began to shake, sending vibrations through the thick soles of their boots. The air a few feet in front of them shimmered, resembling the heat haze above a fire. A small opening slowly materialised, initially the size of one of the buttons on the soldiers' coats, but it grew larger, expanding to the size of a dinner plate.

"Now!" the scientist shouted to the lieutenant. Baumann aimed carefully and threw the pine cone through the emerging window. As their eyes followed the flying pine cone's trajectory, they suddenly saw two people on the other side. The cone landed harmlessly at the feet of a knight in brilliant shining armour, who looked down at it before staring back at the German soldiers in disbelief.

Captain Stahl swiftly drew his Luger pistol, pointing it at the boy standing beside the knight. But before he could pull the trigger, the portal collapsed, concealing the Endless World once again. He cursed loudly, frustrated by another missed opportunity.

"Open it again!" he shouted at the scientists.

"We can't. We need to recalibrate. This was the first time

we observed an object passing through. With our new readings, we should be able to keep the window open for longer and allow a person or two to pass through," the scientist quickly explained.

"Do it!" the captain barked, angrily taking a seat on a nearby log.

CHAPTER 31

*S*eeing the dark captain and his pistol pointed directly at me sent shivers down my spine. The nameless knight swiftly grabbed and pulled me behind him, out of the line of danger. With one hand, he drew his sword from behind his back, and with the other, he produced a small, cylindrical object made of gleaming metal—a miniature flute. He swiftly put it to his mouth and blew, emitting a piercing cry that echoed through the air, reminiscent of a chorus of eagles.

"We must return to the palace at once," the nameless knight exclaimed without hesitation. We quickly mounted his horse and galloped back to the safety of the castle. As we rode, the shrill sound of the whistle continued, reverberating and filling the air like an alarm. Then something remarkable caught my attention. In the sky above, giant birds appeared, resembling birds of prey but the size of men. Their feathers gleamed like polished metal.

"What are those?" I shouted into the nameless knight's ear.

"The winged knights," he shouted back. Despite many

167

swirling in my mind, I realised now was not the time for more questions.

As we approached the bridge to the castle keep, a group of guards formed a blockade at the entrance. They quickly made way for us to pass through. We continued over the bridge, the large wooden doors now firmly shut. As we neared, a shout from above caused the door to creak open slowly. Behind it, a spiked iron gate ascended into the archway, previously hidden from view. We entered the large courtyard, still adorned with warm hues from colourful drapes above but now completely deserted.

We hurried through the courtyard, down the tunnels, and into the Hall of the Brave Ones. We made haste through the now-empty walkways and finally reached the grand throne room. We immediately dismounted, and several guards stepped aside, allowing us to pass.

"Pierre!" My mother's voice resounded through the throne room as we entered. Relief and fury intertwined in her tone. I found it difficult to look at her, knowing I had directly disobeyed her instructions.

"I'm sorry, Mother," I said feebly, consumed by shame for my actions. My plans had certainly not gone as expected, and now I found myself even further from correcting the mistakes that had led to my father's demise.

Ignoring me, she turned her attention to the nameless knight. "What's the emergency?" she asked.

"We have a breach at the monastery portal, Your Majesty," the nameless knight responded loudly and clearly.

"No intrusion has been detected," she replied, her voice carrying a hint of doubt.

"They have opened the portal and threw a pine cone through. It landed harmlessly by my feet, but soldiers from an enemy army were on the other side. I believe that we are moments away from an actual breach," the nameless knight confirmed.

"How?" the queen whispered to herself.

"Mother, they have electrical instruments and have been conducting experiments for weeks now. They—"

"Pierre, you must go and be with your father now," she interrupted crossly. "You need to listen to my words. Your safety is paramount. Leave now." Her firm words filled me with even more guilt. If only I had followed both my father's and mother's instructions, I would not be entangled in this mess. I bowed my head in submission.

"General Thunder!" My mother's commanding voice broke the silence. From a shadow on the other side of the room emerged a large winged knight. General Thunder stood several feet taller than the nameless knight, dressed in armour similar to his, her hair as white as snow, flowing neatly into a single plait. I was in awe. I had never seen a female soldier before—she was magnificent and fierce. But what intrigued me most were the large wings made of majestic golden feathers neatly folded behind her back.

What was she? I pondered in amazement.

"Assemble your regiment in the forest. We have had a partial breach that needs immediate remedy," my mother commanded respectfully.

"Of course, Your Highness," General Thunder replied, bowing low before swiftly exiting the room. I stood there, still staring in disbelief.

"Pierre," my mother's voice broke through my trance. I immediately recalled her instructions and realised I had not yet left.

"I'm sorry, Your Majesty. We'll go now," I began to turn away to leave.

"Wait!" she called out. Rushing down the steps from her

dais, she embraced me. "Be safe," she said with a smile, releasing me. Then, she nodded to the nameless knight.

"My command supersedes his. Take him to his father," she said sternly. The nameless knight bowed low, and we made our way out of the castle and toward the great waterfall.

* * *

WATER THUNDERED AND CRASHED, sending white spray and a fine mist into the air. The bright sunlight illuminated the mist, creating a transient rainbow that appeared and disappeared in the shifting droplets. The waterfall nestled at the end of a valley, and we followed a path along the valley's edge until we reached the base of the falls.

The sound was deafening as the nameless knight helped me down from his horse. "You have to find the portal yourself. I can't help you with that, I'm afraid," he shouted to me above the roar.

I looked around, struggling to focus amidst the constant crashing of water against rocks and pools. Closing my eyes, I tried to remember the technique for finding a portal. But no matter how hard I concentrated, I couldn't sense anything.

"I can't," I shouted back to the knight. "I can't see it! It's too hard to focus here."

A little frustrated, the knight grasped my shoulders and looked directly into my eyes. "Young prince, it doesn't matter what you feel. It matters who you are. You are Prince Pierre, a member of the royal lineage. This secret belongs to you. Use it," he declared, releasing me and returning to his horse. I stared at him for a while, his words echoing in my mind. Locating a portal was very much about feeling, despite my confusion on how to proceed. I began to search the surroundings for a clue, a sign of some sort.

Perching myself on a mossy rock, I gazed into a pool of

water at the base of the falls. The knight's words repeated in my mind—it doesn't matter what you feel, but who you are. I reflected on that, contemplating who I truly was. Just a normal young boy, part of a royal family in a hidden world unknown to others. It sounded absurd, but here I was, in this place. I remembered the people bowing before me, addressing me as majesty. I truly was a prince.

Amidst the thundering water, a faint sound emerged—a distant flute. It carried a curious melody. Intrigued, I followed the gentle song, stepping along the narrow trail toward the edge of the waterfall. As I approached what seemed to be a dead-end, the trail continued behind the cascading water itself. The path opened up like a crescent, allowing travellers to navigate past the waterfall.

The flute's melody faded as I entered the recess behind the waterfall. I glanced back at the nameless knight, expecting him to have heard it, but he remained seated, seemingly preoccupied with something.

The path, carved out from the rocky side, reminded me of the caves I had explored with my father, especially when he first revealed the secret of the portals. Drawing on that memory, I quietly focused and occasionally caught faint hints of the melody—a whisper, an impression in my mind.

I continued to explore the rocky wall with my hands, listening carefully to the song as it fluctuated in my mind. It didn't take long to locate the spot where the hidden music played the loudest. Despite the bizarre nature of the Endless World and its fantastical elements, I didn't question the mysterious music. It had become normal to me.

Confident that I could open the portal, I placed my hands on either side of the spot and, with relative ease, revealed an opening the size of a small window. It opened to almost complete darkness, resembling a tunnel within the wall. Yet, a faint light emanated from within. As my eyes slowly adjusted, I discerned the outline of another door.

Turning to tell the knight about my discovery, I found him standing right behind me, startling me. "Well done, Your Majesty. I knew you'd find it," he said with a smile.

"Goodbye, sir. Thank you for helping me," I began, realising that it might be a long time until we met again.

"Yes, I suppose so. Take care, young prince," he said, bowing low.

"Hey, you never did tell me why you don't have a name," I blurted out, suddenly aware of the lingering mystery. The knight glanced at me, weighing whether or not to explain. Recognising my status, he realised he had little choice.

"I suppose you've found the portal, and your father isn't exactly going anywhere," he conceded before embarking on his tale. We settled on a nearby rock as he recounted to me the story behind his name or, rather, the lack thereof.

* * *

A LONG, long time ago, hundreds of years ago, I used to sail the seven seas as a smuggler or, as some might romantically describe, a pirate.

But life hadn't always been that way for me. I grew up in a small fishing village along the rugged coastline of Cornwall. My father, a hardworking fisherman, had expected me to follow in his footsteps. He would rise before the sun each day, casting his nets into the tumultuous sea and returning with his bountiful catch under the moonlight. It was a tough life, but simple and beautiful in its own way.

My mother, equally resilient, tended to our needs. She nurtured our vegetable garden, stitched our clothing, and wove nets for my father's fishing endeavours. On days when she wasn't toiling away, she would travel long distances, performing domestic work for wealthier families in the nearby area. She worked tirelessly, taking care of my siblings and me, ensuring we had what we needed.

As soon as I could walk, my mother assigned me tasks around the house. I eagerly became her little helper. And as I grew older, just a year or two wiser, my father deemed me ready to join him at sea. I cherished those moments, spending more of my childhood on the ocean than on land.

However, there were days when the winds howled fiercely, and my father would deem it too dangerous for me to accompany him. On such occasions, I would sulk about assisting my mother with her chores, yearning to brave the colossal waves by my father's side.

One fateful day, the sky darkened ominously, and tempestuous clouds swirled in all directions. The sea roared with monstrous waves crashing against the unforgiving rocks, flinging sprays of white foam into the air. In the distance, the clouds took on an eerie purple and black hue, accompanied by the relentless rumble of thunder. Unsurprisingly, my father forbade me from joining him. However, this time, my mother protested vehemently, pleading with him not to set sail at all. But my father, finding her pleas amusing, convinced her that he needed to fish that day. Reluctantly, she allowed him to navigate the treacherous waves, disappearing and reappearing amidst the towering swells.

When my mother and I paused for lunch, we ventured to the cliff edge, hoping to catch a glimpse of my father's boat. The conditions had deteriorated, with ferocious winds making even standing a daunting task. The once-distant dark clouds rapidly advanced toward the shore as lightning strikes crashed down into the churning sea before our eyes. Visibility was scarce, and locating my father's boat proved impossible. Defeated, we trudged back to the shelter of our home.

By evening, the storm unleashed its full fury. Torrential rain and powerful winds lashed our small house relentlessly. Thunder boomed outside, mirroring the turmoil within. Leaks sprouted throughout the dwelling, forcing me to scurry between them, placing pots and pans to contain the spreading water.

When nightfall finally arrived, the worst of the storm had passed. But there was no sign of my father. As we retired for the night, we clung to the hope that he would return by morning. But the sun rose on a tranquil, blue-skied day, the sea calm as a mirror. It was as if the previous tempestuous hours had never transpired. Yet, my father remained absent, and his boat was nowhere to be seen from the shore.

My mother and I hurried down to the secluded cove, the very spot from which my father would set sail. As we reached the small sandy shore, we encountered splintered fragments of wood strewn about, remnants of a shattered vessel. Even without concrete proof, both my mother and I knew it was my father's boat. Overwhelmed with grief, my mother collapsed to the ground, weeping. Despite the calmness of the weather, darkness clouded our spirits that day.

The following days and weeks were extraordinarily difficult. Without the provisions my father would bring, survival became a daily struggle. There were days when hunger gnawed at our empty bellies, and my mother found it increasingly challenging to bear the weight of our dire circumstances.

She started disappearing for longer stretches, leaving us with no knowledge of her whereabouts. My siblings and I were left to fend for ourselves, and I resorted to fishing on an abandoned raft I had stumbled upon while searching for sustenance among the rocks.

Lacking my father's expertise and his sturdy nets, my fishing expeditions were often fruitless. Days would pass before I would manage to catch even a single fish. Meanwhile, my mother's absences grew longer until, eventually, she never returned—or perhaps we didn't stick around long enough to find out. Several weeks of enduring such hardship drove us to make a desperate decision.

My siblings and I made our way to the nearest town, where we became street urchins, surviving on scraps and seeking shelter wherever we could find it. I found solace near a local tavern, lurking in the shadows, for they often discarded decent leftovers. The patrons, aware of my presence, occasionally tossed me a morsel or two, treating me like a stray dog. In their small acts of kindness, I found a semblance of belonging among the company.

As the years passed, I observed a group of young men who frequented the tavern every few weeks. They stood out from the others, their laughter and camaraderie infectious. To my young eyes, they seemed to embody a life of excitement and adventure. As a child of the streets, I had become adept at remaining unseen, a silent observer to the tales shared by the patrons—especially after a few drinks.

Their stories often spoke of mythical creatures spotted at sea or the daring exploits they had undertaken in faraway cities. While much of it seemed embellished or wholly fabricated, it was captivating nevertheless. Among this group of young men, however, I detected hushed conversations and veiled discussions about clandestine activities they wished to conceal. Though I couldn't discern the exact nature of their endeavours, I caught fragments here and there, understanding enough to realise they were involved in something secretive and intriguing.

This knowledge captivated my imagination until the day I summoned the courage to offer my seafaring skills and become a part of whatever they were up to. At first, they dismissed me as a stranger, uninterested in my services. But I persisted, insisting that I could be of assistance every time they returned to the tavern. Finally, they relented, granting me the opportunity to set sail with them. Yet, they kept me at arm's length, separate from their mysterious activities. My role, at least initially, was to fish for them. We journeyed to the northern coast of France, where I was forbidden from joining them once ashore. Instead, I explored the seaside villages and towns alone, patiently awaiting their return from whatever secretive pursuits they were engaged in.

After several months of supplying healthy amounts of fish for the crew, the captain assigned me new tasks beyond fishing. I found myself loading and unloading the goods acquired during our foreign travels as we arrived back in Cornwall. Tasked with storing these goods in tucked-away coves along the shoreline, I couldn't deny that I had suspected their piratical nature all along. Tales of smugglers had circulated in the tavern, and the locals held a mixture of fear and awe whenever they visited. Yet, rather than deterring me, this newfound knowledge drew me deeper into their world.

I relished the opportunity these new tasks provided and earned respect within the crew. Before long, I joined them on their quests along the shore. However, as the years passed and our smuggling operations from France to England became mundane, I grew restless and began seeking ways to amass greater wealth. Instead of venturing all the way to France and spending our own resources on acquiring goods to smuggle, I observed passing vessels carrying legitimate cargo and boats ferrying important individuals with the potential for vast riches. They appeared as easy targets, holding the promise of amassing a greater fortune.

At first, the captain scoffed at my considerations, dismissing them as folly and greed. I had gone from having nothing to feasting and drinking to my heart's content, yet I yearned to risk it all for even more riches. It didn't take much persuasion, as our current operations always went according to plan, and the captain himself grew bored. Amongst these men, myself included, contentment and satisfaction were elusive concepts; our minds were constantly scheming for ways to increase our wealth, consumed by a relentless obsession.

We started by raiding smaller vessels, finding their crews surrendering swiftly, terrified of the consequences if they resisted. The rush of adrenaline was immense, and not only were we making more money than before, but the thrill itself was exhilarating. Eventually, even that became tedious, and we set our sights on larger ships, relishing the prospect of real fights. The crews aboard these vessels were hardy and ready to defend their cargo, making it more challenging to seize their goods. However, we soon honed our skills, and fear ceased to be a factor. We even raised a flag as a warning, proudly signalling our intent to raid.

Our exploits continued, and we accumulated vast riches. We were at the pinnacle of our game, with other boats attempting to flee at the mere sight of our raised black flag. We felt invincible, ruthless, and insatiable—an immensely dangerous combination. Emboldened, we ventured further into the vast ocean, where larger ships traversed their cargo routes. They became our primary targets.

It was during one of these ventures we found ourselves hundreds, if not thousands, of miles from shore when the storm struck. Panic consumed our vessel as dark clouds loomed on the horizon. At that moment, my mind drifted back to the dreadful day when my father went missing, never to return.

The approaching clouds growled like angry beasts as colossal swells lifted our boat to precarious heights before crashing down into deep troughs. Rain lashed down, and the wind whipped the sea's surface, drenching us all. Though our bodies were soaked, our focus remained fixed on keeping our vessel afloat as the tempestuous wind tore through. We were tossed about, powerless to prevent the inevitable. Then, out of nowhere, a colossal wave materialised, swallowing our boat whole.

Some of us perished immediately, while others valiantly fought, desperately swimming back to the surface. But it was futile. Waves crashed upon one another, making escape impossible. Slowly, I succumbed to my demise, surrendering to the darkness of the sea below. In my final moments, my thoughts were of my father, understanding the horrors he must have endured. A profound sense of sorrow and regret enveloped me as I met my terrible end, driven by personal gain rather than the well-being of my loved ones.

For reasons I still do not comprehend, this wasn't the end for me. As my life slipped away, I found myself trapped in a deep slumber, a realm of nothingness where awareness lingered but movement, sight, and thought eluded me.

Gradually, a faint light emerged and with it, a dawning consciousness. I raised my hand to shield my eyes, the brightness uncomfortable after what felt like years of darkness. It was as though I were seeing for the first time in a millennium. Slowly, I became aware of my body, carefully moving my toes and reacquainting myself with my senses.

Lying on a cool, flat stone surface, I struggled to sit up. The effort proved tiresome and arduous. Gradually, my eyes adjusted to the light, revealing a dimly lit chamber. Cobblestone flooring met my gaze, while the walls consisted of large stone blocks. Topped with a small metallic grated window, a simple wooden door allowed a gentle stream of light to flow in. The room was devoid of furnishings, leaving only the stone bricks and my bewildered self.

Propping myself against the opposite wall, I rubbed my

eyes, memories flooding back—my childhood, my days living on the streets, my life as a smuggler, and finally, the catastrophic storm that brought my demise. Questions swirled in my mind. Was I alive? Where was I?

Attempting to stand, my legs betrayed me, and I stumbled, struggling to find my footing. It was as if I had never used these legs before. After a moment, I managed to rise and staggered toward the wooden door and its metallic grate, hoping for a glimpse of what lay beyond.

Peering through the grate, I caught sight of an empty hallway, gently lit by several candles resting in iron holders along the walls. I strained to see farther down the corridor, but my efforts proved futile. Instinctively, I tried the door handle, only to discover it was locked.

The clinking of metallic boots echoed on the cobbled floor, signalling someone's approach. Fear, long dormant, resurfaced as I stood there, uncertain of what lay ahead. Was this my judgment day?

Retreating to the far side of the chamber, I awaited the impending arrival. Keys jingled from the other side of the door, followed by the unlocking of the mechanism. The door swung open, revealing a tall knight adorned in resplendent armour and a crimson cape.

Awe and trepidation rendered me motionless as the knight approached and lifted me up. No words were exchanged as he led me out into the dimly lit hallway, guiding me through what appeared to be a castle keep.

We traversed the corridors silently until we arrived at a majestic throne room, where Her Majesty the Queen awaited. This was not Pierre's mother but a queen from a time long before her reign. I found myself awakened within the Endless World, not as a mere guest, but as a "potential"— someone granted a second chance and the opportunity to reside in the Endless World if they surrendered everything to its cause.

"Welcome to the Endless World," the queen began with elegance. I bowed low, feeling the weight of reverence in this hallowed place. "You have been awarded an opportunity for redemption and a fresh start, should you choose to accept. The judges have deemed it fitting to present you with this choice. What is your answer? Will you live in servitude to the kingdom or venture into the Dark?"

Confusion clouded my mind as I grappled with my surroundings and the identity of this queen. Nonetheless, as I reflected on my life—from the innocent days of my youth to the fateful moment of my demise—a profound sense of sadness filled my heart. I recognised the depths of my poor choices, and though I had once revelled in my actions, they now disgusted me. I yearned to shed the skin of the person I once was and embrace the possibility of redemption. The choice, though presented as such, was clear to me.

"I accept," I trembled, tears of sorrow and joy flowing freely. The acceptance reverberated through the room, solidifying my decision.

"This is fantastic news," the queen responded, elated with my choice. Cheers erupted, knights and members of the royal house celebrating around me. I looked around, bewildered and unsure how to respond.

"They rejoice in your decision to embrace life," the queen declared, noticing my confusion. "You have rejected your former ways and embraced the essence of the Endless World. You are now a citizen of this marvellous place."

As the celebrations subsided, the queen addressed me once more. "There is one thing. Your name has not been revealed to me. What were you called?" Shame washed over me, for my name was the only vestige of my past life.

"I no longer wish to bear that name," I declared, almost as

a plea. "I am no longer that person. I renounce the name I once had; it no longer represents who I am."

"I understand," the queen nodded. "You are now free."

The knight who had escorted me to the throne room stood by my side. "Come, nameless one. Let us depart. The queen has many matters to attend to."

I quickly nodded and bowed low, offering my respect and gratitude to the queen before following the knight.

As we walked, I resolved to become a knight myself, dedicating the rest of my days to serving the cause of good. Though I was not given a new name nor had I thought of one for myself, I became known as the Nameless Knight—a testament to the new beginning I had chosen in the Endless World.

* * *

"THANK YOU," I told the knight sincerely and got up to head back to the portal. "It is a great honour for you to tell me your story."

"The honour is mine." He replied reverently.

I took one long last look at this limitless place and then stepped into the blackened room in the wall. The portal closed immediately behind me, and I was enveloped in darkness.

CHAPTER 32

The outline of the door allowed rays of light to pierce through into this darkened room, or what could more accurately be described as a closet. Soft robes hung on the walls, and as I fumbled about, my hand found the long wooden handle of a broomstick. As my eyes adjusted, I noticed that the robes were clergy wear for a church, perhaps choir cassocks.

Crouching slightly, I peered through the small keyhole, closing one eye to allow for sharper focus. Through the keyhole, I could see the ward filled with injured soldiers and nurses flitting between them, offering water or performing various checks on their patients. The main area of the church had been transformed into a makeshift hospital.

I tried the handle. The door clicked and opened a fraction. I pulled it wider and ventured out into the ward, careful not to get in the way. I scanned the area, trying to catch sight of my father. Looking through the golden orb, I remembered him being roughly situated in the middle. However, from this low vantage point, I couldn't see beyond the beds and pillars.

Keeping out of the way of the nurses, I made my way toward the centre. The soldiers lay in various degrees of distress and injury, some seemingly okay, while others remained completely still, covered in bandages. Every now and then, a groan broke the silence, serving as a grim reminder of the brutality of war. It was an overwhelmingly unpleasant place to be in.

"Hey! Little boy!" A nurse suddenly appeared, shouting at me accusingly. "You're not supposed to be in here!"

"I-I'm sorry, my father is here," I began, my voice trembling.

"Liar! The patients' children are far from here," she retorted, walking toward me and roughly grabbing my ear.

"I'm not! My father is here!" I protested, growing cross. The nurse ignored me, muttering under her breath in annoyance.

Suddenly, a voice called out, "Wait." The nurse reluctantly stopped, still clutching my ear. She turned to face the owner of the voice. "Let me look at the boy."

The nurse sighed in frustration and steered me toward the prone soldiers. "Father!" I called out as soon as he came into view.

"Pierre? My son!" My father responded, starting to clamber out of his bed, his face etched with agony. The nurse immediately let go of me and I rushed to my dad's side.

"No, no, no. You stay in your bed. We've already had to replace your dressings multiple times due to you not resting properly," she scolded him.

I ran to my father's side and held his hand, looking him up and down. Blood-stained bandages covered his wounds. "I'm so sorry," I began. "It's all my fault, I—" But before I could reveal Marc's betrayal and the secrets I must keep, I held my tongue. "It's all my fault," I repeated instead. My father shook his head.

"No," he said softly, clearly fatigued and in pain.

"Get some rest," the nurse commanded again, her gaze turning crossly to me. "I don't know how you got here, but your father needs to be still and not be distracted." She paused for a moment, then added, "Just stay out of the way, okay?" I nodded quickly in response, and she left, apparently satisfied.

"There's so much to tell you," I began again, but suddenly, a man appeared next to us. I looked at him, our eyes meeting, and we stared at each other in silence. He wore plain clothes and almost blended into the environment, but there was a particularly mysterious air about him.

"It's okay," my father said in almost a whisper. "He's my friend. James is from the British military and is here to help us." I looked back at James, his expression unchanged.

"It's okay," my father repeated, sensing my reservation. He squeezed my hand. "You can tell us everything you know. It's very important to give James as much detail as you can—how many soldiers were at the orphanage, anything you might have heard or seen, even if you think it's an unimportant detail."

James took a seat and gestured for me to join him, inviting me to sit and share. And share, I did. I recounted all of my experiences, from arriving in the snow to meeting Alix, the monk, encountering the German soldiers and Captain Stahl with his first lieutenant, discovering the scientists and their quest for the portal secrets, formulating our escape plan, and finally, Marc's betrayal. I shared and remembered it all.

At the end, I looked toward James, still holding onto his sleeve. "Please, sir. I have friends there still. Can you help them? Isabelle is only little. Please," I pleaded.

James looked concerned and nodded at me. He rose from his chair and leaned towards my father. "Michael, I've got everything we'll need," he whispered quietly. He stood, ruffled my hair, and left the church. I watched as the enigmatic man disappeared.

"Dad, I met Mother!" I exclaimed to him, unable to wait any longer to share the news. But my father lay there, fast asleep, the conversation taking its toll on him.

I held his hand, feeling the weight of exhaustion from the recent series of events. I looked about the room, looking at the altar and the stained glass windows. I surveyed the candles and stacks of hymn books and bibles. I offered up prayers for my lost friends still trapped at the orphanage; I pleaded for their safety and for justice. Finally, I closed my eyes and drifted off to sleep, still holding my father's hand firmly in mine.

CHAPTER 33

*T*he sound of a lone bell rang out through the cold air, its echo suppressed by the snow-covered landscape. Isabelle lay in her bed, staring at the ceiling, knowing that the end of the shift had arrived. The marching of boots resonated in the courtyards below, echoing through the hallways inside. The soldiers rotated four or five times a day, and the bell signified a shift change, coinciding with the awakening of the children and monks for the day and for breakfast.

Fire duty had become Isabelle's sole responsibility now, unquestioned and unnoticed by others. Fear had driven the captives to mind their own business, reverting to the same ways they had adopted when Pierre and Isabelle were first brought to this place.

Hopping out of bed, Isabelle made her way down to the food hall, joining the others. She sat next to Thomas, her usually quiet companion, and they began their breakfast ritual.

Several days had passed since they had overheard the captain discussing the portal and their ongoing attempts to open it. Doubt had taken root in Isabelle's heart. Each day, she walked with anticipation, hoping that a commotion would suddenly erupt, signalling the arrival of a rescue operation led by Pierre and an army from his home world. But each day, the sun moved across the sky without any such incident.

Maybe today would be different? Isabelle looked hopefully at the guards in the food hall, wishing they would spring into action in response to a rescuing army. However, they remained motionless, watchful like statues.

One of the soldiers stood and headed towards the door. Isabelle's heart skipped a beat. Could this be it? She tugged on Thomas' elbow, and he turned to her, his mouth full of the same watery oats they had been consuming day in and day out for weeks. His expression remained unfazed.

The soldier opened the door, and another soldier emerged from behind, handing over a small package. The soldier sat back down, fumbling with the package. He pulled something out and handed the package to the other soldier on guard duty. They exchanged items, and the soldier by the door disappeared.

The two soldiers lit their cigarettes and started conversing jovially. Isabelle's heart sank.

"We should prepare for the worst," Thomas said quietly.

His remark, though welcome since he had gone days without saying anything, frustrated Isabelle. She didn't blame his pessimism or lack of hope. Given the dire circumstances and recent events, it was understandable. She looked at her quiet friend, feeling deep compassion stir within her. He may have given up, but she refused to do so. Pierre was still out there somewhere. Although he had gone to another world, surely he would return. She resolved that her preparedness would remain unwavering – that was the one thing still under her control. The day continued as it usually did. The routine bells rang out, signalling the end and beginning of shifts. Fire duty remained uneventful, as always.

As the sun set behind the mountains, Isabelle and Thomas finished lighting and restocking the various fires they had been assigned to. Thomas disappeared to join their evening supper while Isabelle lingered for a few more minutes. She positioned herself in a way that would allow her to respond better if Pierre were to return at that moment. Her stomach growled, urging her to join her friend for dinner. She stood still, listening carefully, before finally leaving with her hungry body and making her way towards the food hall.

She sat with Thomas, and they finished their plain meal in silence. Without incident, they headed back to their dormitory and went to bed.

Isabelle had been wearing her boots to bed, not wanting the hassle of putting them on and dealing with the laces if Pierre were to return in the night. She lay there, staring at the ceiling. Not today, then. She closed her eyes as her mind drifted off to sleep.

In her dreams, Isabelle envisioned a German soldier running down a monastery hallway, his boots echoing loudly along the long candlelit space. He barked urgent commands. Was it happening? He disappeared, fading into darkness as his footsteps quietened. Not this time.

The footsteps sounded again, starting softly and quickly gaining strength like rain on a tin roof. Isabelle bolted upright from her slumber as the sound continued in her waking moments. The noise had invaded her dreaming as noise sometimes does, shaping one's dreams.

The soldier ran past their dorm door and disappeared. Isabelle climbed up to the small window above her bed, using her makeshift step. She couldn't see in the darkness but could hear the soldiers running frantically back and forth, shouting commands and relaying messages. She rushed to Thomas' sleeping form and shook him awake.

"Come on. Something is happening!" she whispered, brimming with excitement. Thomas slowly and reluctantly got up from his bed, putting on his boots and coat.

Without waiting, Isabelle slipped away, silently leaving the slumbering dormitory. Sticking to the shadows, she crept along as quickly as she could, refraining from running to avoid discovery.

She hovered at the end of the hallway, observing the scene. The soldiers all seemed to be outside now. Thomas emerged from the darkness, slightly out of breath, catching up with his friend.

"Something has them all in a fluster," she whispered excitedly.

They carefully made their way outside, avoiding detection. The Germans were bustling about, shifting positions in the courtyard. A truck's engine revved and made its way across the track right in front of the pair. They hid perfectly still inside one of the garden's hedgerows, watching as the large tires rolled across the muddy snow, spraying soggy ice towards them. The truck reached the gate, trampling without concern. The soldiers guarding the gate quickly opened it, allowing the truck to pass through as it disappeared into the field beyond.

With the coast clear, Isabelle and Thomas made their way to Alix's cabin and hid among the wood stores as more soldiers came and went.

They waited silently as another military truck trundled through. Isabelle peeked around the corner as the guards opened the gate and hopped onto the back of the truck as it departed. Wide-eyed, she glanced back at Thomas.

"It's clear," she whispered loudly. Thomas joined her side, and they cautiously approached the now vacant gate. The truck continued on the other side of the field, its headlights illuminating the woods beyond.

They hovered by the open gate, unsure of how to proceed. Venturing into the woods would surely lead to capture. They felt dangerously exposed where they stood.

"Come on," Isabelle beckoned her friend. "Let's go this way. We can remain out of sight and might be able to get close enough to see what's going on."

They cut a new path on the other side of the field and slowly made their way to the edge of the woods. They crept into a cold ditch and crawled quietly toward the noisy soldiers just ahead. Recognising the gravity of the situation, they moved cautiously. The sounds of German voices grew nearer as Isabelle and Thomas crested the side of the ditch and observed the unfolding scene.

Two scientists busied themselves with various lengths and coils of wire. The captain, dressed in black, stood against a tree, observing while puffing on his pipe. The first lieutenant paced back and forth, commanding a line of soldiers with their rifles raised. Other soldiers emptied trucks filled with large crates containing various supplies. There were more soldiers present than Isabelle had ever seen. They must have called for reinforcements.

A pair of soldiers carried a large crate over to the captain. They opened it, revealing a folding desk and a large electrical device. It was a telephone. They assembled it and left it with the captain.

Suddenly, the first lieutenant grabbed one of his soldiers and screamed at him.

"I need you to pay attention, you imbecile! They could open the door on their side anytime and have a waiting army. The wretched boy was with an armed knight of some sort. When we open it, you need to start firing. Understood!?" He released the soldier and then continued to pace like a crazed maniac.

Isabelle turned to Thomas in shock, finding him nodding. It confirmed that Pierre was on the other side and had a soldier of his own. They could have an army ready to swoop in and destroy these unwelcome devils.

They continued to watch the scene unfold. The captain was busy on the phone, likely speaking to his superiors. Something significant was happening. They were preparing for a major battle.

CHAPTER 34

*T*he queen of the Endless World sat, fixated upon her swirling golden orb, mesmerised by a sight that brought deep joy to her heart. Her expression transcended mere laughter or smiles but instead carried a profound sense of contentment that endured through the highs and lows.

At this moment, tears welled in her eyes as she peered fondly at her little prince, her son, and his father, her beloved husband. They were finally safe. She settled back into her ornate throne, releasing a sigh of relief and gratitude.

The rhythmic sound of hooves clapping against the hard floor resonated in the throne room as the Nameless knight returned. The queen gently wiped away her tears and composed herself.

"Your Royal Highness," the knight said in greeting, bowing low.

"Well done, my knight," she replied, acknowledging his loyalty. The knight stood and approached the dais. Although her cheeks were now dry, the queen's emotions remained apparent. Uncertain of how best to comfort her, the knight attempted to say something consoling.

"Your Majesty, time may seem to move slowly, but they will find their permanent home here with you once their time on Earth is over." The queen nodded, acknowledging the truth in her loyal knight's words. "And, I'm sure there will be countless windows where you can see them from time to time." Added the knight, gesturing to the orb.

To this remark, the queen seemed to disagree. Perplexed, the knight waited, anticipating an explanation.

The queen turned and retrieved something from behind her—a pristine purple cushion typically used to present precious jewellery. Carefully holding it, she revealed a small golden hammer resting at its centre. Despite resembling a child's toy, its solid gold construction and exquisite crafts-manship indicated otherwise.

"What is it?" the knight asked in awe, quickly adding, "Your Majesty."

Smiling, the queen began to explain, "This was a wedding gift given to my great-great-great grandfather by the moun-tain elves. It is made of the same material as the seeing orb. In ancient times, there were many orbs, but over time, the rest have vanished. This is the last known seeing orb in existence."

She held the hammer up to the orb, demonstrating their resemblance to the knight.

"See you soon, my dear princes," she whispered, kissing her fingers and gently placing them on the orb's surface. In response to her touch, the clouds swirled. With her other hand, she swung the little hammer hard and true, striking the side of the golden sphere.

A melodic note rang out, resonating like the delicate chime of a wine glass. The orb shimmered, sending ripples cascading across its surface, resembling a stone dropped into a still pond. It repeated this twice more before returning to stillness.

The knight stood in shock, disbelief etched on his face. The orb exploded before he could question the queen's actions, shattering into several large pieces.

"Your Majesty! Why did you do that?" the knight asked, kneeling down to gather the precious fragments.

"Take these pieces. Bring them to General Thunder; she will distribute them among our winged knights," the queen instructed.

"Of course, Your Majesty," the knight obediently replied. He hesitated, attempting to frame a question from his confusion, but he knew it was not the time to ask too many questions. His perplexity was evident to anyone who glanced at him.

"This war that rages on Earth employs various weaponry. They have built flying machines armed with cannons and guns, although they are no match for our winged knights. We shall never enter Earth ourselves. However, with these shards, our winged knights can observe the aerial battles and guide and aid those fighting for good. They reflect sunlight, appearing as flashes of light on Earth, leading their pilots to the evil forces attempting to breach our sacred lands."

"A great sacrifice, Your Majesty," the knight acknowledged, though the destruction of the last known orb seemed almost reckless.

"We have little choice now. If the secret of the portals is discovered, not only will the Endless World be in severe jeopardy, but Earth and all other realms will also be. Where corruption enters, sorrow and destruction follow," the queen explained.

The knight bowed, walking away toward his waiting

steed, carrying the shards carefully. Questions lingered in his mind, but he knew his place and the importance of the task entrusted to him.

* * *

A MILITARY ENCAMPMENT had been established by the royal guard, encircling the hidden portal. General Thunder stood tall among the guards, surrounded by several other imposing winged knights.

The Nameless knight approached at a gallop, the golden shards clinking in the bag attached to his back. Dismounting swiftly, he presented the bag and its contents to the commanding general.

"What is this, knight?" General Thunder inquired.

"Ma'am, these are Elvish gold shards from the queen's seeing orb. She broke it so that your regiment can use them to observe Earth from the skies, directing pilots and aiding in the aerial battles," the knight explained with reverence.

The general nodded, accepting the bag. Delicately, she distributed the shards among the winged knights, who handling them with great care, secured the shards within their armour.

General Thunder handed the last shard to the Nameless knight. She gripped his shoulder, a gesture of solidarity, before releasing a piercing call like an eagle. The other winged knights responded in kind, launching into the sky as one, disappearing beyond the treetop canopy. Falling branches and pine needles showered the ground underneath.

The knight joined the ranks of the other guardsmen, unsheathing his sword with a satisfying ringing sound. He raised it carefully, and his focus honed in on the area where he had last seen the German captain and his first lieutenant.

A shimmer filled the air before the royal guard as the ground trembled beneath their metallic boots.

"READY!" Shouted the commander of the royal guard.

CHAPTER 35

*A*s the minutes turned into hours, Isabelle and Thomas found the icy bitter cold increasingly uncomfortable. Meanwhile, the animated lieutenant grew more energetic and angry; a sense of urgency filled the air.

"Reinforcements," Thomas whispered quietly as several more trucks appeared, forming a larger camp with tents in the field. Isabelle and Thomas huddled close to each other, desperately trying to retain their diminishing warmth.

Excitement surged as the scientists started to open the portal. Isabelle tightened her grip on Thomas' hand. The air before them began to shift and shimmer while the crazed lieutenant berated his troops, demanding their readiness. He stood with his arm outstretched, clutching his pistol tightly, pointing at the shimmering air, prepared for what lay beyond.

A loud whirring sound, like a rapidly spinning fan, filled the air, followed by a crashing noise reminiscent of shattering glass. Cursing and angry outbursts erupted from the scientists and Captain Stahl. The first lieutenant, Baumann, couldn't contain his fury. Stahl stared at him and shouted, "Keep it together, Baumann," shaking his head in disgust.

Isabelle felt a wave of relief wash over her, quickly followed by a wave of dread as the inevitable conflict still loomed ahead. She whispered, "Can you hear that?" looking to Thomas for a response. He nodded slowly. A distant hum, resembling the drone of bees passing nearby, filled the air.

"Planes," Thomas mouthed, his voice barely audible. The Germans also began to notice, gazing up towards the source of the sound. They scattered like startled cockroaches, diving for cover and extinguishing the campfires, switching off all lights. The planes flew directly overhead, the once-distant hum now thunderous. Dark shapes and silhouettes obstructed the cloud-covered sky.

The planes flew past the monastery, circling back. Suddenly, a brilliant burst of light emerged from the darkness, directly above the camped soldiers. It lasted only a moment before disappearing. Shortly after, another mysterious light appeared this time high above in the skies.

Isabelle and Thomas stared up at these inexplicable lights as they continued to flash sporadically above and all around them. "What is it?" Isabelle whispered, her voice barely audible.

"I don't know, but I have a feeling we need to take cover," Thomas replied quickly, crouching down to the ground.

The planes returned, now flying lower. The whining engines signalled their descent, triggering panic and confusion in the wood as their supposedly hidden location became known to the Allied pilots.

Sudden gunfire erupted from the field as men started shooting wildly into the air. Isabelle and Thomas cowered in the ditch, covering their ears from the deafening sounds.

A high-pitched whistle pierced the air, growing louder and louder. BOOM! An explosion struck the firing soldiers in the field, but Isabelle and Thomas couldn't see it. Shocked beyond belief, they were surrounded by falling ice, dirt, and bits of tree. Seconds later, another dreadful whistling sound began. Huddling close, they did everything they could to protect themselves. The second explosion deafened their ears, leaving them with only ringing.

"Get it open now!" Captain Stahl screamed, urging the scientists and soldiers to respond to his command. The strange flashes of light resumed, illuminating the night sky as hundreds of parachutes floated down. Shouts from the soldiers intensified as they unleashed gunfire upon the new threat.

In response, more gunfire illuminated the wood. Isabelle and Thomas remained prone at the bottom of the ditch, splinters falling all around them. They squeezed their eyes shut, waiting for the nightmare to end.

"Get ready!" the first lieutenant berated his men, determined to open the portal again. Gunfire rang out above them as they sought cover.

"Stay where you are, you cowards!" the lieutenant continued, steadfast with his pistol raised once more.

The ground beneath the wood started to vibrate. The air shimmered, and Isabelle crept to the top of the ditch, daring to steal a glance. On the other side of the opening portal, trees in warm, sunny shade began to appear faintly.

"Hold the line!" the frothing lieutenant barked.

The trees came into focus as the portal continued to open, revealing knights in brilliant armour bearing shields, swords, battle axes, and all sorts of menacing weapons. They stood waiting, watching from the other side, their presence contrasting the dark, cold wood.

"Hold the line!" came a valiant shout from beyond.

CHAPTER 36

*P*ools of warm light gently filtered through the dense canopy of tall trees in the wood. The tranquillity of the forest was interrupted only by the melodic calls of birds and the soft rustling of squirrels scurrying about.

The Nameless knight and his brothers-in-arms stood in the midst of the wood, motionless like poised statues. Their weapons were at the ready, reflecting their razor-sharp focus and exceptional discipline. High above, winged knights soared in formation, already engaged in their own battles.

Before them, a portal began to open, revealing a grim and desolate scene. The knight's commander beckoned his men to prepare themselves, bracing for whatever might emerge from the other side.

Contrary to the Endless World's serene and peaceful nature, figures clad in military fatigues holding guns appeared like ghostly apparitions. "Have courage!" came the command.

Gripping their swords tight in response, the knights braced themselves for the impending onslaught. The tranquil atmosphere of the Endless World was now infiltrated by the sounds of war from Earth, corrupting its calm and quiet.

Suddenly, a loud shout echoed from the dark world beyond. "Now!"

Machine gun fire erupted with a thunderous roar, accompanied by blinding flashes of light. The bullets tore through the air, shattering through trees and crashing into the regiment of knights defending their world.

Fortunately, their armour, forged from metal found only in the Endless World, offered protection from the bullets. While Earth's metal could shield against ricochets, it would eventually rust and corrode. However, the Endless World's metal possessed superior durability and resisted such decay. Despite this advantage, the force of the bullets still caused the knights to stagger backwards, their agile movements compromised by weak points in their armour.

Determined, the fallen knights rose to their feet, grabbing shields to protect themselves from the onslaught. With fluid precision, some sheathed their swords and drew bows from behind their backs. Arrows swiftly flew through the narrow portal, striking the German soldiers and forcing them back.

The volley of arrows continued, repelling the German forces. "Get it closed!" shouted the knight commander.

With an arrow, the nameless knight pulled back and, ready to fire, aimed through the chaotic and dark gap, searching for a target that could collapse the portal. Gunfire and explosions illuminated the scenes of despair, obscuring his view of how the portal had been opened.

A soldier suddenly charged toward the knight, arm poised to launch a grenade through the portal. Swiftly, the nameless knight dispatched an arrow, piercing the man's arm and pinning it to a nearby tree. The soldier cried out, dropping the grenade to his side. The knight instinctively raised his arm to shield his face as the ensuing explosion sent dirt and debris crashing through the portal.

As the dust began to settle, the knight lowered his arm, only to find another soldier charging towards him. This soldier was being propelled forward by the first lieutenant, whose rabid face was locked onto the nameless knight. They crossed the threshold into the Endless World as bullets whizzed past, causing the knights to seek cover.

Emerging proudly behind them, the tall captain, dressed in black, strode forward, accompanied by more soldiers bursting through the portal on either side.

The nameless knight swiftly plucked an arrow from his quiver, but his bow was destroyed before he could release it. Captain Stahl grinned as smoke curled gently from the end of his pistol.

In an instant, the knight raised his sword, pointing it at the oncoming soldier with the lieutenant close behind. Stahl continued firing shots, striking the knight's armour and causing him to stumble, dropping his sword.

The deafening sound of gunfire echoed through the warm wood, bouncing off the valley sides. Arrows and bullets filled the air as the two sides exchanged shots.

Struggling to regain his footing, the nameless knight reached for his fallen sword. However, he was forcefully kicked back by the first lieutenant, who pressed his boot down hard on the knight's armoured chest. Smirking sadistically, Captain Stahl emerged from behind the lieutenant.

"Where's the boy?" the first lieutenant cruelly demanded, his anger evident.

"You fools," the knight responded defiantly.

Anger flashed across Baumann's face, incensed by the knight's defiance. The captain joined in with laughter. "Fools? Ha! You're not very smart, are you?" scoffed Captain Stahl.

Explosions continued from beyond the portal, spraying ice and debris into the Endless World. The Allies were gaining ground, crushing the remaining German force.

Stahl pushed his lieutenant aside and knelt down, pointing his pistol at the knight's face through a narrow opening in his helmet.

Helpless and prone, the knight lay at the mercy of the deranged commander. He looked past the barrel of the pistol, gazing into Stahl's eyes. Instead of seeing a fierce, dangerous man, he felt a pang of pity, recognising a lonely soul who had long strayed from the path, seeking approval from those who never cared for him.

"Where's the boy?" Stahl asked, his voice laced with anger.

The knight would never allow these men near the young prince.

Pressing his pistol harder against the knight's brow, Stahl awaited his answer.

"Take your hands away from my knight!" a sudden voice resounded from behind the royal guard.

The queen, adorned in resplendent golden armour, rode in on horseback. Stahl and his lieutenant looked up, stunned by the brilliance of the golden figure approaching them. Baumann stepped forward, raising his pistol and firing successive rounds at the queen. The bullets ricocheted harmlessly off her armour, accompanied by dull metallic sounds.

Undeterred, the queen continued her advance, raising the white staff she carried in her hand. With a loud scream, she pointed the tip of the ancient wooden stick at Stahl and Baumann. A massive burst of invisible energy erupted from the staff, sending the two men hurtling backwards, unable to resist the powerful force emanating from the queen's staff.

As she circled around on her horse, the queen unleashed her royal guard, ousting the remaining German soldiers from her domain. Witnessing their leaders being tossed about by an invisible force, the German soldiers hurriedly retreated back through the portal, gladly returning to the arms of their enemies.

Before the last soldier could escape to Earth, the queen fired another blast of force, propelling them into the air and through the portal. Swiftly dismounting her horse, she leapt to the ground and slammed her staff into the earth, causing a shockwave to ripple outward. In an instant, the portal vanished, concealing the Endless World from the cruel scenes on Earth.

She hurried over to the nameless knight, who remained kneeling, recovering from the bullets fired at him. "Brave knight, are you okay?" she inquired, evidently concerned in her voice.

The knight held up a hand, signalling that he would recover. The queen knelt beside him and placed her hand on his shoulder.

"Thank you," she said graciously. "Thanks to you, our young Pierre is safe again, far away from any danger."

CHAPTER 37

I watched the door to the clergy room almost daily as I sat there bored with my father. It had been several weeks since I had rejoined him, grateful for our reunion but with little else to occupy my young mind. The nurses took care of the wounded men, and I had become adept at staying out of their way. Exploring the church and inventing imaginary games occupied my time somewhat, but the door to the clergy room beckoned me. Behind it lay a path that led to a warm wood, beyond which lay a much colder wood. A short walk from there would take me to the mountainous orphanage—the ancient monastery where my friends were held captive.

The ache inside my heart grew as uncertainty gnawed within me. Were they safe? What had transpired since I left that place? I glanced at my father, his injuries a grave reminder of my ill-considered actions. I vowed never to make the same mistakes again, but even with that resolution, peace eluded me. I felt the heavy weight of the pain I had caused.

My thoughts drifted to Isabelle, and I hoped she was safe.

Once this was all over, I vowed I would find her, ensure her reunion with her family, and make a promise to protect her like a brother.

* * *

CONTRARY TO OUR EXPECTATIONS, my father miraculously survived his severe injuries. It was several more weeks before my father recovered enough for the kind nurses to allow us to leave the makeshift hospital and continue his recovery at home. But where was home? We were a long way from our southern holding, and the war still raged on. Returning there seemed unwise, given my father's fragile health. Fortunately, a generous family from a village twenty miles east offered us a place to stay. We settled there until France was liberated, which finally made it safe for us to return to our home in the South.

Returning home felt surreal. Everything remained untouched, save for the dust and cobwebs that had accumulated in our absence. After a thorough cleaning, we re-established our lives. I couldn't help but notice how everything appeared smaller than I remembered. My childhood bedroom seemed diminished, and the kitchen was tiny. It was then that I realised just how much I must have grown. Memories flooded my mind, and I longed for the innocence and purity of those bygone days.

My father resumed his carpentry business, and as I grew older, he took me under his wing, teaching me the art of crafting beautiful wardrobes, chairs, and other commission pieces that came our way. The war had been a harrowing experience, tearing families apart and leaving behind great atrocities. It was difficult to fathom a return to normalcy, yet here I was, reunited with my father, finding solace in the simple joys of life.

I became intentional in my approach to life, cherishing each moment and learning as much as I could from my father. We would visit the lakes, the place where he had first revealed the secret of the portals to me, as often as possible. In those quiet moments, we would discuss the wonders of the Endless World, and our most cherished conversations revolved around my mother. It brought him delight that I had met her, and in this sanctuary, we could freely speak of her.

As the years passed, my father's war injuries became increasingly burdensome as age took its toll. His slight limp, a constant reminder of my past mistakes, was accompanied by growing pain. With each passing day, his ability to enjoy his work as a carpenter diminished. Eventually, he relinquished most of his craft, and I gradually took over the business, following in his footsteps.

I continued the family legacy while my father pursued other hobbies like oil painting. We navigated life together for several more years, enduring bitter winters in the mountains where the cold seemed to gnaw away at my father's body. He aged rapidly during those times, his vitality fading. I blamed his war injuries, comparing his declining health to other men his age who remained fit and able.

One winter afternoon, his death came abruptly. Having completed most of my daily duties, I made us both a cup of coffee and brought it to his bedroom, where he rested. I assumed he was merely sleeping, leaving the coffee on a tray beside his bed, confident he would awaken soon. But as I turned to leave, I caught a glimpse of his face and noticed a faint blueness on his lips. I stopped in my tracks, calling out to him.

"Father!" I repeated, my voice filled with desperation, refusing to accept the truth.

Resigned to his passing, I sat on his bed, gently caressing

his peaceful face. Overwhelmed with grief, I sobbed, mourning deeply. I knew I would see him again in our true home, but it offered little solace for the sadness I felt. It was my actions that led to his injury, robbing him of joy and ultimately shortening his years on Earth.

Night after night, I lay in bed, haunted by memories of the monastery, tormented by thoughts of what might have been had I been more cautious and kept our family's portal magic a secret. I continued living out my days in my father's holding, marrying a lovely girl from the nearby village. Together, we had a son and a daughter. On their eighteenth birthdays, I took them to the familiar caves, just as my father had done for me, revealing their true identities and calling on Earth.

I never did fulfil my vow to visit the orphanage, the place where Isabelle and Thomas were held captive. By the time it became safe, the war had long ended, and the evacuees had likely returned to their homes. I made inquiries here and there, hoping to find Isabelle, but her whereabouts remained a mystery. I could not recall her family name, which added to my frustration. I did learn that Thomas' father perished during the war, but Thomas himself never returned home.

It saddened me that I couldn't discover their fates, but I took solace in the knowledge that we would be reunited in the Endless World. I lived a long and fulfilling life, passing away peacefully in my sleep. One moment, I closed my eyes in my earthly bed, and the next, I awoke in the royal palace of the Endless World.

The nameless knight greeted me in my chamber where I lay, escorting me to my eagerly awaiting parents. We celebrated with a grand feast, indulging in the finest meats. I regaled my mother and father with tales of my wife, our beautiful children, and their grandchildren.

* * *

BEING BACK in the Endless World was wondrous, and I relished the time spent with Alix and Eric in the Hall of Brave Ones. I dedicated hours to learning from the elders, eager to unravel the mysteries of this realm and beyond. Yet, despite the joyous reunion, a lingering turmoil troubled my heart, burdened by deep-rooted shame. During one such meeting with the elders, one of them confronted me about it.

"Prince Pierre, Your Royal Highness, there seems to be a lingering stench about you," the elder remarked bluntly, his words cutting to the core.

I chuckled, appreciating his directness but also feeling sombre, knowing he had touched upon something deep within.

"Yes," I replied, "it hasn't quite let me go."

"Has it not let you go, or have you not let go of it?" The elder's response disarmed me, reframing my perspective.

"I betrayed the secret of this place. I betrayed my father, and he suffered greatly because of me. I endangered my friends and put the whole of the Endless World at risk," I confessed, the weight of my guilt heavy upon me.

The elder smirked slightly, his eyes wise and knowing. "This place was never truly at risk. I concede that your actions could have led to dire consequences, but it would have taken more than what transpired to truly threaten the Endless World. Have you seen Alix and Eric? How do they appear to you?"

"They are in a good place now, but they endured great hardships because of me," I responded, my voice tinged with remorse.

"Perhaps, but they were also greatly rewarded," the elder remarked, challenging my perspective.

His words echoed in my mind, and I pondered them

deeply. He was right. What did my father genuinely think about the hardships he endured and the injuries he sustained? It hadn't even occurred to me to ask him. In that instant, I knew I had to see my father. I expressed my gratitude to the elder and rushed back to my father's house.

Knocking on his workshop door, I found my father without injury, his beloved craft in his hands once more.

"Come in," he invited, and I entered, taking a seat beside him. I shared my conversation with the elder, explaining the burden on my heart.

My father listened attentively, nodding along. I hesitated, then summoned the courage to ask him about his thoughts regarding his injuries and the struggles he endured because of me during his time on earth.

"My son," he said fondly, "I would do anything to keep you safe, even those challenges all over again. But let me tell you, those German soldiers would have found their way to that place, with or without you. And as for my injuries, Pierre, it was indeed difficult, but the times we spent together when you helped me were the most precious moments of my life on Earth. Despite my failing body, I was filled with joy working alongside you. I wouldn't trade those moments for anything."

As my father spoke those words, a weight lifted off my shoulders, freeing me from the burden of guilt and shame. He taught me what it meant to be a son, and in that lesson, I found forgiveness—for myself and for my mistakes of the past.

CHAPTER 38

*S*tahl, his first lieutenant, and the remainder of their unit were led away by the Allied forces. Moments before, the captors had become the captives. The mysterious James, the friend of Pierre's father, led the Allied forces in their mission. He commanded the immediate capture of the scientists and the swift destruction of their instruments and any paraphernalia remaining from their experiments. The soldiers quickly rigged the area with explosives and led the captives out of the wood.

Isabelle and Thomas remained hidden while the brutal scenes had unfolded before them. They were shocked and amazed by the arrival of the Allied soldiers and the mysterious flashes of light that seemed to have helped them navigate to this place.

"What should we do?" Isabelle whispered to her friend. Thomas stared back, unsure. He shifted uncomfortably, causing a stick beneath him to snap. Immediately, a British soldier ran over.

"Don't move!" he screamed, pointing his rifle at them. Realising the two terrified children before him, he lowered his gun. "Got some children here! Get me a blanket," he shouted to the soldiers behind him.

They were quickly taken care of and given a hot chocolate each to warm up. Isabelle recounted the events to the allied soldiers and gestured toward the monastery in the distance, still full of children and monks.

They led a group of men to the orphanage, where the occupants carefully emerged from their hiding places. Unaware that it was now safe, they reserved any further movements. Isabelle and Thomas, clothed in warm blankets and holding their steaming drinks, were signs that they were indeed safe. That being said, the children were still guarded, and some even retreated while others stepped forward, eyeing the prospect of a warm, comforting beverage.

One of the elderly monks came over to shake hands with one of the allied soldiers. The silent exchange symbolised the liberation of the monastery. Other monks followed, offering their thanks to the friendly soldiers.

A bell rang out as the monastery came to life, and monks and children busied themselves with various duties, culminating in a gathering in the food hall and a special dinner was served to everyone present. Seated at the tables were a mix of soldiers, monks, and children. The soldiers offered small pieces of chocolate to show kindness to the more timid ones. Some played card games, while at one table, a soldier performed magic card tricks, providing a form of entertainment not seen in this place ever before.

* * *

THE SOLDIERS REMAINED at the orphanage until the end of the war and beyond due to the events of the portal. The children who had been evacuated to the mountainous monastery were taken back to the train station and reunited with their families. Some sadly lost a father or an older sibling from the war and returned to a grieving mother, while others, like Thomas, had lost all their family. His father had been lost to another conflict, that of alcohol. The events were hard enough for most people, and those already vulnerable, like Thomas and Eric's father, were pushed harshly over the edge. Some would point out it was his decision; no one forced him to drink. But as we now know, people are easily led astray and will believe in something poisonous if a quick comfort is offered.

Once it was known to be safe, children were able to return to their homes. But now, instead of responding to the news with jealous scowls, hateful words, and gestures, everyone would stand and erupt with clapping and cheering. Isabelle loved this and pondered that had Pierre been present, he would have beamed with delight.

Thomas and the other orphans were offered residence at another orphanage since they had nowhere to go. He accepted his fate with indifference; the prospect didn't excite him much, but he had no other available choice.

When Isabelle's name was called out, the hall erupted in cheer as was now custom. Isabelle was propelled forward to go and claim her prize. She turned to Thomas, who watched, smiling and clapping with the others. She lingered, not wanting to say goodbye to her close friend. Reluctantly, she was led out of the food hall and taken to an awaiting horse-led coach in the courtyard. Her possessions had been packed into her simple bag and satchel.

She stopped and refused to go any further.

"No," she said quietly to the monk escorting her to the awaiting coach.

"Pardon?" the elderly monk said, leaning down to be able to hear better.

"My friend Thomas, he's one of the orphans. I'd like him

to come with me. We can house him; my family has a big house," she said clearly and confidently. The monk looked at her in bewilderment for a while before nodding and disappearing back into the monastery, leaving Isabelle alone with the pair of horses and the coach.

She looked about the quiet courtyard for what felt like an eternity, down toward Alix's cabin and the field beyond. It was very quiet now. Reflecting on the events that had played out at this place, she felt a sense of sadness to now be leaving. She had come here in the first place under terrible circumstances, yet Pierre had taught a way of life that enabled times of enjoyment. Suddenly, the door opened behind her, and the ancient monk reappeared, walking slowly back toward her. She eagerly looked beyond, but no one was following. The monk looked at her as he passed and gave her a simple smile and nod before carefully climbing up to the coach driver's box. Isabelle took one last look at the open door before saying goodbye and climbing into the awaiting coach herself. She hoped Thomas would accept but thought it might be too much for him. She cried nonetheless, and the monk called to his horses to start the precarious descent down the cobbled road toward the train station.

"Wait! Wait!" came a shout. The monk pulled the reins as the horses whinnied in unison. Isabelle opened the small coach door and shot out to greet Thomas, who appeared from the darkened hallway.

"Room for one more?" he said, smiling. The monk nodded and waited. Isabelle beamed with delight.

"You came!" she exclaimed. "But you don't have your things?" she continued, concerned by his lack of belongings.

"I don't really have anything," he replied, pausing, and then said, "I think it's time for a new chapter for me." Smiling, they both climbed in, and the monk led them away from the orphanage.

* * *

Thomas stayed with Isabelle's family until he went on as an apprentice for a building merchant at the age of eighteen. He had a wonderful time with his new family and rediscovered life. He came back to visit in his mid-twenties, now a young, established, and successful man. Isabelle herself had gone on to study Interior Design at a prestigious school in Paris.

Thomas asked Isabelle's father for her hand in marriage, at which he was most delighted. Her father nodded cheerfully, and Isabelle and Thomas got married and moved to Paris. Isabelle was highly successful, designing the wealthiest of the wealthy's apartments and chateaus. Thomas, too, was successful in building new developments in Paris.

They rarely spoke about the events at the orphanage. It was a painful memory for them both. Occasionally, something would remind them, and they would talk about the good things. For Isabelle, it was whenever it snowed, and the morning frost took her back to dorm duty and traipsing across the icy courtyards to get to the various dormitories. For Thomas, it was that of his brother, who always looked out for him. He now recognised that his brother's behaviour wasn't ideal, but he saw that he had copied how their father had treated them. It was the moment that Eric sacrificed his life so that Pierre could escape. This made Thomas incredibly proud of his older brother. He hadn't thought about the events that happened, perhaps for years, before he allowed his mind to visit the memory. It was very painful for him, yet he had somehow discovered a way to frame it where he thought about it as an acknowledgement of the bravery exhibited.

They never visited the monastery or attempted to connect with Pierre, believing he had returned to his unseen world, never to return.

As you now know, this was not the case. Yet their paths never crossed again, well, while they were on Earth. It would come as no surprise that Isabelle and Thomas made their way to the Endless World, just as Pierre knew they would. Thomas was reunited with Eric and enjoyed exploring the beautiful gardens that Eric had cultivated within the Hall of the Brave Ones.

In the royal palace, the most magnificent food awaited, as I'm sure you can now imagine. Like the great hall at the monastery, this too had beautiful stained glass windows reaching from the floor up high to the tall ceilings.

Large feasts were a regular occurrence in the royal palace, with much jubilant celebration and performances. A special table was always prepared by Prince Pierre for himself, Isabelle, Thomas, Eric, and Alix. It is rare for a group of people to share such a deep connection as this group did. Many toasts were shared, many stories told, with tears and laughter abounding.

On their table, Pierre always set up an extra place. The plate would remain empty, and the cutlery untouched. At first, no one said anything, allowing Pierre to have his own reasons for this. Until Eric, in his classic blunt fashion, asked Pierre directly about it.

"Your Majesty, who is the place for?"

"You can just call me Pierre, you know," said Pierre, chastising his close friend, then answering the question. "We have had a missing party member. I hope one day he'll join us."

CHAPTER 39

*B*irdsong erupted joyfully as dawn ushered in a new day. The sun's gentle rays cast a warm glow as it rose from behind the mountains.

Nestled in the rocky mountainside, the ancient monastery had stood for millennia. The once lively halls were now inhabited by only a handful of monks who remained.

In a cosy log cabin, a monk sat at a small desk, bathed in sunlight streaming through the tiny windows. He immersed himself in ancient scrolls and scriptures, pondering their hidden meanings. Despite the early morning chorus of birds, the monk had already risen for the day. Sleep had become elusive in his old age. Standing up from his desk, he peered out the cabin window to survey the courtyards outside. Two monks dressed in humble garb made their way to the orchards to gather ripe apples. The monastery had adapted to post-war life, finding sustenance and support through selling produce and goods such as apple stew and jams.

Nodding silently to the passing monks, he opened the cabin door and walked toward the wood stores. After a long, harsh winter, the wood stock was running low. Today would be arduous, but the lone monk found solace in the labour ahead. He entered the great hall first, savouring his simple meal of oats and water, a staple he had grown to appreciate over the past sixty years.

With his belly full, he gathered his axe and knife, crossing the field to the woods on the other side. Cows grazed peacefully, paying no mind to the monk as he passed by. The short walk left the old man fatigued until he found respite in the shade of the trees.

Felling trees had become an art for him, maintaining a balance between harvesting new ones and ensuring a steady supply for the monastery's needs. Though minimal in recent times, the monk wished to secure an abundant firewood supply. He carefully selected a tree, calculating the precise spot for it to fall. With a sharpened axe in hand, he swung, striking the trunk's lower section. Wood chips flew as he attacked the tree, and within minutes, it creaked and groaned, falling exactly where he had planned. Unsheathing his knife, he knelt down, laboriously removing small branches, and meticulously discarding leaves. As he prepared to make the final cut, a snapping stick startled him. Looking up, he caught sight of a deer meandering through the woods, closely followed by another. The pair vanished into the wilderness, leaving the monk's gaze fixed upon an ancient tree, its interior blackened by a long-ago lightning strike and subsequent fire.

Kneeling there, his face darkened as painful memories flooded his mind. The events that occurred sixty years prior still haunted him. Though he resumed his task, his sombre mood lingered, an unfortunate recurrence in the ageing monk's life. Sleep, when it did come, was plagued by nightmares, denying him true rest.

Having finished trimming the tree trunk, ready to saw

and chop it into firewood, he took a sip from his water bottle and temporarily set aside his tools. He made his way back to the monastery for lunch, sitting alone as he ate his simple meal. Afterwards, he returned to the field and entered the woods. Embracing his solitude, he grasped the saw and began cutting the trunk into manageable pieces. The task would likely occupy him for the remainder of the day. He worked diligently, neither rushing nor hesitating.

During a short break, he reached into his bag and pulled out an apple, slicing a piece off and savouring its flavour. Again, a sudden snap of a branch made him turn. He expected to see the two deer once again, but to his surprise, there was nothing there. Puzzled, he glanced around, but whatever had caused the sound had vanished before he could identify it.

As he prepared to cut another slice from the apple, a delicate snowflake drifted gently past his shoulder, landing on the smooth blade of his knife, quickly melting. Mystified, he stared at the small drop of water, blinking as if trying to reaffirm reality. Several more snowflakes materialised around him, and he turned, feeling the snow tickling his face and exposed arms. In disbelief, he stood, dropping the knife and apple from his hands as a figure emerged before him through a hidden portal. Clad in garments suited for wintry flurries, the figure bore intricate details on closer inspection. A sword rested at their side, their hand gripping its hilt.

The monk stood frozen, shocked by the unexpected presence. Snow blew into the warm wood, melting upon contact with the monk's sandals and the ground beneath him. With eyes fixed on the ominous figure, he sensed his fate. Deep down, he had suspected this day would eventually come, and now he faced it head-on. Bending at the waist, he pleaded to the figure before him, "Please, make it quick."

In response, the figure drew its sword, its resounding

ring echoing in the air. Yet, instead of striking, they gently placed the blade on the monk's shoulder. A stern voice commanded, "Rise." The monk slowly straightened up, meeting the figure's gaze. As he stared into those ancient eyes, the present acceptance of his fate momentarily wavered. It had been a very long time since he had looked into those eyes. The figure unravelled the scarf wrapped around their neck and lower face, revealing their identity.

"Pierre," he said, astonished.

"Marc," Pierre replied.

"You've come for justice?" Marc posed the question more as a statement than an inquiry.

"I have," Pierre replied simply. Marc nodded in acceptance.

"I always knew this day would come. I wasn't sure if you had made it safely away. I accept my fate, Pierre. Do as you see fit," Marc said, gesturing toward the sword still held by Pierre.

"Let us sit and talk first," Pierre sheathed his sword, motioning to where he and his father once sat. "You are right, Marc. Your actions led to a terrible outcome, causing the deaths of both Alix and Eric."

As Pierre spoke, tears welled up in the monk's eyes.

"I know. I've regretted that day ever since. I'm truly sorry for the horrible things I did. I betrayed your trust, Pierre."

"We will address that. But first, let's talk about Alix and Eric. Your actions played a part in their demise," Pierre continued. Marc sobbed, the weight of his guilt over-whelming him. "They are in a better place now, having departed from this world and joined the Endless World. Their bravery has been honoured."

Marc looked toward the portal, a smile playing on his lips. "That's good."

"You should also know that they hold no resentment

toward you. They understand what you did and have chosen to forgive you," Pierre reassured him, placing a hand on the old monk's shoulder.

Marc looked at Pierre, uncertain of what to say. Pierre's touch provided a glimmer of reassurance.

"On the matter of your betrayal of myself, Isabelle, and the many others who suffered at the hands of those terrible men," Pierre continued.

Marc nodded, acknowledging Pierre's words. "Yes, I must pay for what I've done."

"You should also know that Isabelle, Thomas, and I forgive you. You were an orphan who lost his way. While we don't excuse your actions, we no longer seek retribution," Pierre explained.

"But you said you came for justice," Marc retorted.

"Yes, and justice has been served. The choice is now yours. You can come with me to the Endless World. You will never be able to return here, but it means you must forgive yourself. If that's something you cannot do, you can stay here and continue your life at the monastery. Before you decide, though, consider that you've spent the last sixty years carrying this heavy burden. I've come here to tell you to set it down. Come with me, old friend," Pierre offered.

"I... I can't. It doesn't feel right. I am a guilty man," Marc repeated.

"The guilt, the shame, they are just yours now. We no longer hold anything against you. Let it go, Marc. Forgive yourself and come with me to my world," Pierre urged.

Marc surveyed the woods, contemplating his options. No one had ever spoken to him of their forgiveness. He had blamed himself for all the misfortunes that surrounded him. Carefully considering Pierre's words, he realised that it didn't feel like justice.

"I can't," Marc finally said.

"I really had hoped you could," Pierre sighed, patting his old friend on the shoulder. Opening the portal with a slight flick of his hand, snow rushed into the warm wood. Pierre wrapped his scarf back over his face and stepped into his home, raising his hand to close the doorway behind him.

"Wait!" the monk called out. Pierre froze, his arm still raised. Marc stared into the frozen, Endless World beyond, his heart pounding. Deep down, he couldn't ignore the stirring deep within him, pulling him towards what he knew to be his true home. And at that moment, as he laid eyes on the Endless World, he let go of his past guilt and shame, which faded away to nothingness, just like the snowflakes blowing into the wood melting upon touching the warmth of Earth.

"I'll come if you'll have me," Marc called out. A wide grin spread across Pierre's face as he stepped aside, welcoming his old friend. He patted Marc on the back, his voice filled with affection.

"Welcome home," he said.

ABOUT THE AUTHOR

Matthew J. Swarbrick lives with his family near the South Downs in West Sussex, UK.

Despite being a software engineer by trade, Matthew enjoys creating story experiences and started the journey of writing around 2010 when the concept of The Orphan Prince came to him in a dream. The story developed over the following few weeks and, over the following years, was turned into a novel.

Printed in Great Britain
by Amazon